Would My
Fortune Cookie Lie?

Would My Fortune Cookie Lie?

by Stella Pevsner

Clarion Books
New York

Clarion Books
a Houghton Mifflin Company imprint
215 Park Avenue South, New York, NY 10003
Copyright © 1996 by Stella Pevsner

Text is set in 12/16-point Kuenstler.

For information about this and other Houghton Mifflin trade
and reference books and multimedia products, visit The Bookstore at
Houghton Mifflin on the World Wide Web at
(http://www.hmco.com/trade/).

Printed in the U.S.A.

Library of Congress Cataloging-in-Publication Data

Pevsner, Stella.
Would my fortune cookie lie? / by Stella Pevsner.
p. cm.
Summary: While worrying that her mom is plotting to move the
family from their Chicago home, thirteen-year-old Alexis also
wonders about the mysterious young man who seems to be
shadowing her and her friend.
ISBN 0-395-73082-1
[1. Moving, Household—Fiction.   2. Brothers and sisters—Fiction.
3. Family life—Fiction.   4. Mystery and detective stories.]   I. Title.
PZ7.P44815Wo   1996   [Fic]—dc20   95-36720
CIP
AC

BP   10   9   8   7   6   5   4   3   2   1

For Alexis Canfield
and Jane Tran

CHAPTER 1

"Suzy thinks she's being shadowed," I said at the dinner table one August night.

"Suzy *what*?" Dad asked.

"Being shadowed," my brother Tyler repeated.

I went on. "When we were walking home from the library today she said she thought this guy was tailing her."

"Tailing her," Tyler echoed. His seven-and-a-half-year-old mind believes that repeating my words is wildly funny and at the same time irritating. He's only half right.

"Good heavens, shadowing someone could be serious!" my mom said. "Suzy's mother should get an injunction, prevent the person from stalking. That's a serious business."

Everything's pretty serious to my mom, who, as a court reporter, spends a lot of time recording the stories of the city's biggest criminals. It's made her cynical and suspicious. I thought I'd better backtrack before Mom got on the phone with Suzy's mother and turned this into a major issue.

"Actually," I said, "Suzy was probably just kidding around when she said it."

"When she said it," Tyler echoed.

"Being shadowed is not to be taken lightly," Mom insisted.

With the dreamy look on his face that made some people say, "Isn't he adorable?" my brother began reciting "I have a little shadow that goes in and out with me, And what can be the use of him is more than I can see. . . ."

"Why, darling, that's so clever," Mom said. "Did you just make it up?"

"Well. . . ." Tyler's eyes blinked behind his little round glasses.

"It's a poem, Mother," I said, "by Robert Louis Stevenson. An old, *well-known* poem." I'm sure Dad had read it to Tyler, or even recited it many times from memory.

Mom wasn't a bit embarrassed by her show of ignorance. Poetry, to her, was a waste of time. "To get back to this shadowing situation—" she began.

"Lorraine," my father interrupted, "let it go. As Alexis just said, Suzy was probably kidding around. You know Suzy. Never a dull moment with her."

"That's right," I agreed. "If nothing's going on, she dreams up something."

"Dreams up something," Tyler repeated.

"Will you stop that!" I clenched my fork and held it next to his upper arm.

"Assault with a deadly weapon!" Tyler yelped. "Cuff her, Mom!"

Dad sighed. "Both of you stop. I've got a grinding headache and I have to work tonight, here at home."

Tyler's black button eyes flashed dollar signs. "I'll help, Dad!"

It isn't that Tyler is such an unselfish little glob. It's that Dad, copy chief in an ad agency, sometimes pays us to help him think of ideas for kid-related products. I got paid bigtime—twenty bucks—last month for a rap session with Dad, just for talking about why kids like or dislike certain soft drinks. From talking with me, he came up with an ad campaign idea. This only happens once in a while, though.

"It's nothing you guys can help with," Dad said now. "I have to write an explanation of some research we did, and draw conclusions."

"Sounds boring," I said.

"Boring," Tyler repeated in a whispery voice. I ignored him.

I sometimes feel that I, Alexis Banning Dawson, have been placed wrongly in this family. Perhaps I was adopted. There was just me for a number of years, then miracle of miracles, Tyler appeared on the scene. I know he was born to this family because my six-year-old self saw Mom in the carrying, if not delivering, process.

I'm nothing like Mom. She has dark blond hair, thick, permed, and pulled back, hazel eyes, and a very positive manner. She never read me nursery rhymes or fairy tales when I was little. It was always books like *I Go to the Dentist* or *Fun with Sand*, which was supposed to get me interested in sand castles because we were going to a lakeside cottage for a week. She made it sound like a school project, and that turned me off.

When I was older, she'd actually read aloud a few pages at a time of transcript from court cases. It was her way of checking her material and putting me to sleep at the same time.

My dad, Harvey, is totally different from Mom. They were raised in the same suburb and started dating in high school. The rest, as they say, is history. But like history, with its battles, my parents have conflicts all over the place.

Just last week, for example, I was awakened by their voices in the living room, not too loud at first, but getting stronger by the minute. My stomach started cramping as I picked up words and phrases: "You've never cared how I felt about it!" I heard Mom say. And then Dad answered, "That's not true. We both agreed—" And Mom interrupted with, "I may have agreed at the time, but that doesn't mean I can't change my mind." "You know it would be hard on the children," Dad said. "The children? They'd get used to it." Then their voices lowered as they came down the hall, went into their room, and closed the door.

I wanted to hear more, yet I didn't. Were they

talking about divorce? It didn't really sound like it, but what else could it be that would be hard on the children?

As I mentioned, Dad's with an advertising agency. He's no more off the hinges, I guess, than the other people who work in his office. I've visited a couple of times, and Dad's even let me sit in some sessions where they kick around ideas for TV commercials. If you think what you see on the screen is bad, you should hear some of the ones that don't make it. Dad's ideas are often the best ones, and I'm not being prejudiced when I say that.

Still, if he tries out a slogan on me at home and I say it's dumb, he'll try it out on Suzy. If she laughs, he'll tell me, "See, Alexis, you're getting jaded. Suzy likes it." If she makes a face, though, or rolls her eyes, he'll comment, "Okay. I get the message."

When my family moved to this apartment building about six years ago, Suzy was already living here. I met her in the elevator one day—we were both going downstairs to the lobby for our mail.

"Hi! You're new here, aren't you?" she said in her rippling voice. "I'm glad there's another girl my age in the building."

I was shy, and just smiled.

"I'm Suzy Wing," she said. "My grandma calls me 'Suzie Wong.'" At the time that made no sense to me because I didn't know *The World of Suzie Wong* was the name of an old movie.

"What's your name?" she asked as I stood there, stupidly, saying nothing.

"Alexis Dawson," I mumbled. And then brilliantly thought of something to say. "We live in 824."

"We're 702. That's neat! We can run up and down the stairs and not have to wait for the elevator when we visit back and forth."

I was dazzled by her easy acceptance of me. In the suburbs we'd moved from, I'd had plenty of friends in the second grade. The friendships had developed slowly, though, because I wasn't exactly outgoing. Now this Suzy took it for granted that we'd become visiting-each-other buddies just on the basis of living in the same building. That's all I took it for at the time, close living arrangements, but later on Suzy revealed she'd liked me on sight. "You looked so *good*," she said.

"Good! Oh, yuck."

Suzy laughed. "I don't mean goody-good. I mean real. Like . . . I don't know. I just liked you. Isn't that a reason?" Then she said, in a fakey voice, rapidly blinking her eyes, "Why did you like me on sight?"

"I didn't. I thought you were ugly, weird, and stupid."

Suzy laughed. "Aside from that?"

"Actually, I was in awe of you. You looked so exotic."

"Exotic? Don't you mean *Asian*?"

"That too. But your hair was so long and shiny and black."

"How about yours? Just as long and shiny, only strawberry blond."

Now that Suzy and I are going into eighth grade, we sometimes talk of that first chance meeting.

"We were so keyed up," Suzy recalls. "Remember? First we went to your apartment and announced to your mom that we were new best friends, and then we ran down the steps to my apartment and told my grandma. My mother wasn't home at the time."

"I'll never forget your grandmother," I said, "hunched in front of the TV, watching her soap and waving us away."

"Good. You are friends," she had said. "Go drink some tea. Or Pepsi. Don't bother me with your silly talk right now."

I had glanced at Suzy, but she wasn't the least bit offended by this dismissal. The little gray-haired woman leaned toward the TV, muttering, "Do not go on that sailing boat with Brad, Jessica. He is too mean. Wants to throw you to fishes!"

She was wearing traditional Chinese clothes: black cotton pants and a floral top with frog fasteners. On her feet, however, were red and white Reeboks, which rather blew the image of Pearl Buck's *The Good Earth*, parts of which we had read at school.

"Should your grandmother be sitting so close to the TV?" I asked Suzy.

"No. But she thinks the people on the show can't

hear her if she sits way across the room," Suzy said, shrugging.

As time went on, I knew that when I visited Suzy during daytime TV it was as if she and I were alone in the apartment. At other times, though, her grandma was quite friendly and surprisingly talkative. I guess she got a little lonesome with both Suzy and her mother gone most of the day—that's why she took such an interest in the TV soaps. Grandma Lily can tell you down to the last detail what Tiffany and Stephen or Talia and Charmaine and Derek are up to.

"Oh, that Talia! Such a bad woman!" Grandmother said just today. "She is playing fast and loose with Derek. Trying to take him away from Charmaine, who is so sick from last implant."

"That's awful," I said. "Maybe Derek will come to his senses and wise up that Talia's just after his lakefront property."

"No! That is not Derek with property. That is Bradley from other show, 'World Beneath Blue Skies.'"

"Oh, right!" I said. "Are you going to write him— Derek—and warn him about Talia?" Grandma Lily kept the U.S. Postal Service in business with her letters to the stars of the shows. The fact that she never received a reply didn't daunt her.

"I think I must wait a few days, see what happens next. I am now more worried about Tangerine Trent who is about to marry her own father-in-law. Big mistake, I think."

"Maybe she really loves him," I ventured.

"Love! Ha! Stir-fry love. Easy to do, fast, forget very soon."

I wondered if Suzy's grandmother had said the same thing about Suzy's parents. According to Suzy, they'd married soon after meeting, but the romance had quickly cooled and they'd gotten divorced when Suzy was about two years old.

Her grandmother had left the home of Suzy's two unmarried aunts in Chinatown to come keep house and take care of the toddler. Even though Suzy didn't exactly need watching anymore, her grandmother happily stayed on. She liked living in the apartment and she adored Suzy, although she criticized her sloppy ways.

"What do you think?" she would say. "I have nothing to do all day but pick up your clothes and hang up?"

"I know you're very busy," Suzy said soothingly. "What happened to Charmaine today? Did those cheekbone implants finally take?"

"Oh!" Grandma Lily sadly shook her head. "Not good. More trouble with the doctor now. He put in some wrong bones. From a goat, I think."

Suzy and I looked at each other. We really didn't want to get into the case history. Suzy would hear it all at dinner anyway, when Grandma Lily brought her daughter up to date.

Suzy's mom works at an import shop at the Merchandise Mart. She consults with decorators who are looking for Asian artware for luxury homes and offices. I think it's a high-stress job, especially when shipments are late coming from overseas or when goods are damaged. Mrs. Wing doesn't complain about it, though. She always manages to look and act serene.

Not like my mom. When she has a bad day in court, watch out!

Dad and I have learned how to keep quiet and not rattle her. But Tyler doesn't know enough to shut up. Just yesterday, when Mom was carrying on about a long and boring trial and how overworked she was, my brother said in his dense way, "Then why don't you just quit?"

"Quit?" Mom yelped. "Quit? Don't think I wouldn't like to. But then who would give this family all of the little extras that it has gotten used to?"

"That's true," Tyler said. "I would miss having food and blankets and things."

"That's not what she's talking about," I said, giving my brother a little shove. "Come on, let's go to your room. I'll play a game of whatever with you."

"Candyland," he said, walking along with me. "But 'Lexis, Suzy's mother works to buy food and things for them."

"Well, yes," I agreed. "But that's because Suzy doesn't have a father."

"She *has* one, stupid. He just isn't here to work and live with them. I don't know why he would go away. Suzy's mother is so nice and pretty. Why would anyone go away?"

"I don't know, Tyler, and it's really none of our business."

"Do you think our dad would just go away, poof?" Tyler tried to snap his fingers.

"Of course not."

"How do you know that?"

Actually, I didn't know. It seemed to me that my parents were arguing more than ever. Would the day come when they would call a time-out? A permanent one?

"They're not the type that would get a divorce," I said.

Tyler tilted his head and thought about it. Then he brightened. "Okay. I get to start the game."

He was convinced by my words. Now I only wished I could convince myself.

CHAPTER 2

The next afternoon Suzy and I were walking home from ballet class, and I was complaining about it being too hot in August to spin around on your toes, when Suzy suddenly said, "He's back. That guy!"

"Where? Where?" I looked behind us. "There's no one there, mite brain. Only Becky and Sharleen."

Suzy stopped, put a hand on my arm to support herself, and raised a foot to look at the bottom of her shoe, as if gum or something was stuck there.

"Now what?" I asked.

"Look over my shoulder."

"All right. What do I see? Apartment buildings."

"Not him?"

"Not anybody. Look for yourself."

Suzy, both feet now on the ground, looked. "He's gone. But he was there. I swear he was!"

"Describe him."

"Tall, thin, dark hair. Kind of cute, just from the glimpses I've had of him." Suzy flipped back her hair with her free right hand.

"It's probably one of your many admirers," I suggested. "Crazy in love with you, dying for just the glimmer of a smile, hoping that once school starts, you'll meet in the hall. . . ."

"I don't think so. This isn't a kid. It's an older guy."

A little warning shiver went through me. This *was* the city after all. Weird things happened all the time, as my mother so often pointed out. "Suzy, I think you should tell someone about it."

She laughed. "What would I tell? I keep seeing a guy?"

"How many times have you?"

She shrugged. "Three or four times. Let's give it a rest, okay?"

"Okay." It occurred to me that Suzy was dramatizing something that could be a coincidence. It might never happen again. "What're you doing this weekend?"

"I have to go with my mom to Chinatown to see my aunt. Want to come along?"

"Don't I wish. We're going to the suburbs. It's my grandmother's birthday. Duh."

I'm never out-and-out thrilled about going to Medsville, which I call Deadsville. It's okay being around Grandma and Grandpa Dawson. Both of them treat me like a rational being, meaning that they take it for granted I can understand anything they talk about. The entire tone changes, though, when my cousins are around. Since they live right next door, they're often around.

Corliss, who's a year older than I am, acts as though she's been in high school all her life and she can barely remember slow, pokey junior high. She goes on about kids I've never met and their wild, almost-out-of-bounds behavior, remarking that if she were a writer, she'd do a sitcom based on them.

Around our grandparents, Corliss puts on a fakey cheerful voice as though she were addressing people deep into senility.

Once, after Corliss had left, I asked Grandma Greta if Corliss came over often when we weren't there.

"No," she said, and looked as though she was about to add *thank goodness* but thought better of it.

My cousin Kelsey, who's eleven, likes to hang around Corliss and me. When we come around to boy talk, an all-time favorite subject of Corliss, she'll tell Kelsey to go play with Tyler.

If Kelsey won't go, Corliss starts talking about algebra until her sister gets bored enough to leave.

❦❦❦❦

Since Dad had to go to the agency on Saturday to put some finishing touches on an ad campaign, he didn't drive to Medsville with us. "I'll catch a train as soon as I can and call you from the station," he said.

On the drive out, Tyler, sitting in front with Mom, asked if we could stop at Burger King.

"Tyler," Mom said, "your grandmother's going to have lunch ready."

"If it's her birthday we should take her out," Tyler said. "To someplace like—"

"People have different tastes," Mom interrupted. "Not everyone enjoys the same thing."

"Yeah," Tyler said, twisting beneath the seat belt to fling a glance at me. "Like stupid Suzy eating that yucky Chinese sushi."

"Sushi," I said, "is a Japanese delicacy, Mr. Ignorance. Suzy is Chinese. And she's not, for your information, stupid either."

"Oh? She says she's being shadowed. That's really stupid."

"It is not! She is!"

I caught Mom's glance in the rearview mirror and instantly knew I shouldn't have blurted that out.

"Alexis," Mom said, "what makes you think someone's following her? Have you actually seen the man—boy—whatever he is?"

I felt trapped. "Not exactly. But I was with her when she saw him."

"Saw him," Tyler echoed.

"Don't you think she's being dramatic? Playing mind games with you?" Mom asked.

I sensed I should go along with this option, but at

the same time I had to be loyal to my friend. "It's what she says," I muttered.

"She says," Tyler repeated.

Mom was studying me in the mirror again. I looked out the window.

A police car swerved around us, red lights flashing, and pulled over the car in front of us.

"Wow!" Tyler shouted, stretching to see who was in the car. "Get a look, Mom. Maybe you'll see that guy in court!"

"I don't work in traffic court," Mom said.

"Just with murderers and muggers, right?"

"More or less," Mom said. "But we don't need to talk about it."

Nevertheless, it got both of them off the subject of Suzy, and for that I was grateful. In a way, I wished it was just something Suzy had imagined, but that would make Tyler right. On the other hand, if it was true, that wasn't so good either.

❦❦❦❦

I like my Grandma Greta. She's quite tall and big, but still not fat. Her hair is a mixture of gray and black, and she wears it straight, with bangs. I think the style is called Peter Pan. Most women her age have perms and frizz, but Grandma's straight, non-fussy style suits her. Grandma Greta's eyes are brown, and when she looks at you, she really looks. Her voice is strong and husky.

"Well, here you are," she said as we trooped in the front door. "I'd ask what the occasion is, but I guess it's because I invited you to lunch." She was wearing her navy blue silk dress with the white collar and floppy bow.

"It's your birthday," Tyler said. "Did you forget?"

"No, honey, I didn't forget." She turned to Mom. "When will Harvey be able to join us?"

"It depends on how long it takes him to finish up some work on the new ad campaign. It's due early next week."

"Advertising's such a crazy business," Grandma Greta said, pulling a casserole out of the oven. "The way I look at it, it's just high-class lying."

"But Grandma," Tyler exclaimed, "the brands Dad writes about really *are* better than the other brands."

Grandma laughed as she took the hot dish into the dining room. "I guess you're a convinced consumer."

Grandpa Mac came in from the yard with a bowl of tomatoes he'd just picked from the garden. He's as tall as Grandma, but thin. His hair is thin, too, and his eyes blink a lot behind thick glasses. He hugged Mom and me and asked Tyler if he'd done the driving. He asks that every time, and Tyler always explains he's not old enough.

Grandpa, Tyler, and I wandered into the dining room, but then I went back to the kitchen to see if there was something I could do. I heard Mom say, "Greta, I'm not sure I want to rent to them again. Their lease is up at the end of September, and I've been thinking . . ." She saw me and stopped. "Yes, Alexis?"

"Should I carry in something?"

Mom grabbed a few paper napkins and handed them to me. "Here."

Grandma looked a bit puzzled. We both knew there were cloth napkins already on the table. I took the hint, though, and left, but I paused behind the door long enough to hear Mom say, "Do you think it would be crazy for us to move out here and live in the house ourselves?"

I nearly dropped from shock. *Move out here? Our family?*

I stood rooted, wondering if I should slam into the kitchen and confront Mom, or just wait and listen. Before I could decide, Grandpa called me over to ask my opinion of a poem he'd composed for Grandma's birthday. "Is it too wacky, do you think, Alexis?"

I skimmed the lines. "It's fine." My thoughts were still on what I'd overheard. "She'll love it." Both of my grandparents write poetry. I think they met when they worked together on a college literary magazine.

Mom and Grandma Greta came in then, and we sat down to eat.

Lunch was the way it usually was when Grandpa Mac and Tyler were together.

Tyler started out. "Grandpa, if you give me a quarter, I can tell you the date without even looking at it."

Grandpa Mac gave him a mock frown. "You trying to tell me you're psychic?"

"Just do it."

Grandpa fished out a quarter, laid it on the table, and covered it with his hand. "Okay, what's the date?"

"Today's August the fourteenth."

"What?"

Tyler laughed hysterically. "I didn't say I knew the date on the quarter!"

"Wow." Grandpa shook his head. "You sure fooled me."

Grandma Greta laughed but Mom just sighed. Tyler had pulled the same thing on Dad just last night, but it had been a dime then. The stakes had gotten higher.

"Give the quarter back," Mom said to Tyler.

"No, no, let him keep it," Grandpa said. "Next time I'll be smarter, and he won't get me." He always said that.

After lunch Mom said she was going to drive to the rental house and check it out. She invited me along, but I refused.

When she'd driven off, Grandma asked me if the house brought back sad memories. I guess she meant about my other grandparents, Mom's folks. They'd lived there until two years ago when they'd died in a freak boating accident on a trip overseas. Mom grew up in that house, and of course we'd visited there a lot.

"It reminds me of my other Grandpa and Grandma," I admitted.

"Of course it does, honey," Grandma Greta said, putting an arm around my shoulder.

"I think Mom should have sold the house when she inherited it," I said. I'd heard Dad suggest that. "Instead of renting it out."

"Well, I guess it was hard for her to let go."

I wanted to ask Grandma about what I'd overheard, but I knew she'd just put me off. She was very careful about keeping confidences. I'd always admired that, but right now I wished she had a weaker character.

Later on Grandpa picked up Dad at the station. Then when Mom got back, we all went next door to my cousins' for dinner. Aunt Jenny—Dad's sister— had baked a birthday cake for Grandma. Uncle Ben was there too, but as usual said next to nothing.

It had always seemed great to me to have both sets of grandparents and my uncle and aunt bunched together in Medsville. I had loved driving there from our own nearby suburb, Winterlake, especially around the holidays. But it wouldn't be quite so wonderful, I thought, to actually live there all the time.

Among other negatives there was Corliss who, tonight, was going on about a great new teen shop in the mall that had a TV monitor you could use to check your looks. Instead of asking "Don't they have mirrors?" I tuned her out so I could tune in what Mom was saying. All I caught was, ". . . determined not to renew their lease. They've let the place run down. It'll all have to be repainted."

"Just as well to get rid of the tenants," Grandpa said. "Fix the house up, and you can raise the rent. It's worth more than you've been getting."

"Well . . . if it comes to that. We'll see." Mom glanced at Dad but he took no notice.

He knows what Mom has in mind, I thought. *And he's against it.*

I pushed my food around on the plate. If I took another mouthful, it wouldn't get past the lump in my throat.

Dad, don't let her do it! Be strong! Don't let her get her way this time! But I knew from experience that in a battle with Mom, Dad almost always lost.

CHAPTER 3

Mom and Dad kept up what I call artificial talk on the way home. Tyler was asleep, even though it wasn't quite dark yet. I looked out the car window at the suburban houses until we got to the toll road, and then there wasn't much to look at at all. No neighborhoods, no tall buildings. Just landscape, messed up with strip malls and factories.

Was Mom seriously thinking of hoisting the family out here to Deadsville? I suspected she was. Mom isn't the kind to talk about actions she doesn't fully intend to take.

But what about Dad? I knew he'd be against it. He loved living in the city. He went to symphonies (alone, or sometimes with me) and to plays, dragging Mom along. He went sailing on Lake Michigan in the summer, on the boat he co-owned with friends. He'd miss all that if we lived in Medsville. He could still do those things, I guess, but it wouldn't be easy.

As for me . . . ! The thought of being separated from Suzy was more than I could bear. It would be like cutting apart Siamese twins. I didn't want to live with the other half of me missing.

Why now, after all these years, did Mom want to move back to the burbs? Wouldn't she hate commuting to the city whenever she had a court reporting job? For Dad it would be even worse, trying to meet train schedules—or forced to go by car because of his erratic hours and having to fight traffic on the toll roads.

Maybe Mom worried about Tyler. She drove him to school now, but he had to make it home on his own. Did Mom's job make her think the streets were crawling with perverts on the prowl for her little darling?

A sudden thought stabbed me. *Suzy's being shadowed.* Oh, man! How could I have been so stupid to blurt that out? At the time I'd thought it quirky, entertaining, and yes, funny. Something to share with the family. But Mom, paranoid by nature and by job, took it seriously. If that was it, if my saying those words had gotten Mom started on this moving mission, I'd never forgive myself.

Dad suddenly turned up the volume on the radio. "Recognize this number, Alexis?" His eyes met mine in the rearview mirror.

"Stravinsky's *Firebird.*" Dad had taken me to see the ballet last year. "We dance to part of it in ballet class," I added.

"You and Suzy going to be in the *Nutcracker* again this Christmas?"

"I guess we'll try out."

Mom moaned softly. Even though she took turns with Suzy's mom, driving us to rehearsals and then to the many performances at McCormick Place, it was always tough on her.

"You'll make it," Dad said.

Mom turned. "I should think you'd be tired of repeating your performance year after year."

"We get better parts each time."

"I mean doing the *Nutcracker* itself." She gave a little laugh. "I get tired just watching it. The same old story and the same dances, too, as far as I can tell."

"It's a classic."

"Well, I know it's a classic, thank you very much. But that doesn't mean it doesn't get boring."

"Dad can drive us then. Or we can take a cab."

"Alexis, I wasn't saying—oh, never mind. I can see you're in one of your moods."

Thanks to you, I thought.

There wasn't much talk on the rest of the drive home. When we got there I went straight to my room. I didn't even call Suzy. She'd know by my tone there was something wrong, and I didn't feel up to talking about it. Maybe nothing would happen. Maybe the idea of moving would just go away.

❧❧❧❧

"I wonder what's the matter with Elizabeth," Suzy said as we walked into Kramer's Snack Shoppe a couple of days later. "The way she almost lost it in class today."

"Madame was really ticked at her—but then, did you notice she let up after the break, when they had that little talk in the corner?"

"Maybe Elizabeth's got problems." Suzy said. "Maybe her cat died, or—"

"She doesn't have a cat."

"Okay, bad choice. Maybe she has to undergo surgery—"

"Suzy, have you been watching the soaps with your grandma?"

"Sometimes in the summer I do. So sue me. Anyway, they do get you in touch with human problems."

"Oh, give me a break."

"Come on! People do have problems, even though *your* life is trouble free!"

I almost blurted out the thing that had been on my mind since last Saturday in the suburbs. But though I'd been on the alert, I hadn't picked up any more dropped bits of information. There was no point in mentioning it to Suzy yet and getting her all stirred up. Let her go on thinking my life was pure heaven.

We were sitting at a booth in Kramer's, waiting for our Cokes, when suddenly Suzy said, "Oh, wow, I don't believe it!"

"What?"

Suzy was facing the room. "Elizabeth there. No! Don't look!"

"You're always doing this to me," I complained. "Carrying on about something and then telling me not to turn around and look. What's Elizabeth doing?"

"It's not—oh!" Suzy hunched down as far as she could.

"What? What? If you don't tell me, I swear I'm going to turn anyway!"

"It's that guy talking to her, and they're looking this way." Suzy bent over the Coke and sucked up half of it in one gulp.

"Who's 'that guy'? Do I know him?"

"Of course not. It's the one who's been shadowing me!"

"No! Is he staring straight at you?" I wondered if Suzy was in danger, but in Kramer's that hardly seemed likely.

Suzy took a quick look. "No, he's standing at the booth by Elizabeth and the girl she's with . . . Katie? But he's facing this way."

"You know what I'd do?" I said. "Go over and ask him what gives. What's his prob."

"You would not. Besides . . . Hey, maybe he's a friend of Elizabeth's."

"Or a serial killer who stalks young girls," I suggested.

"Now you sound like your mom after a hard day in court. Oh, he's leaving. Don't look."

"Don't *you* look," I said. "He's walking right past the front window and he's . . . he's glancing at us. Now he's gone on by. He's kind of cute, Suzy."

"How old would you say?"

"I'm not sure. Older than high school."

"Did he look Asian to you?"

"I barely saw him, Suzy. Maybe a little around the eyes. I don't know."

"I'm going to ask Elizabeth and get this thing settled," Suzy said, scooting out of the booth.

She came back in just a few minutes and shrugged. "Liz doesn't know him. She said he asked if she knew how to get to the Cubs Stadium and she told him she didn't have a clue."

"That's all?"

"No. He asked her what our names were, and if she thought we'd know."

I just stared at Suzy, waiting for her to go on.

"She gave him our names, but said we wouldn't know from zilch about the Cubs or how to get to Wrigley Field."

"I think I could have told him what bus to take," I said.

Suzy exhaled a huge sigh. "That's not the point! *He asked for our names!* Doesn't that seem strange to you?"

It did, actually, but I hated to admit it. "He probably didn't want to come up and say, 'Hey, you! Know how to get to the stadium?'"

Suzy shook her head. "You can be so dense. He could have found out from any guy how to get there. Why would he ask Elizabeth? I'm telling you. Just to get our names!"

I had to admit she was probably on track.

Who was this strange person anyway? And why was he following us—or rather, Suzy? What was the connection?

I had no idea. I didn't know what to think. But one thing I did know. I wasn't going to tell my parents about this near encounter. No way.

CHAPTER 4

"Don't be so glum," Suzy said. "With any luck, Tyler will jump the ditch and a lion will eat him up."

We were on our way to the Lincoln Park Zoo, which is on the North Side of Chicago, near the lake. From where we live it's only about three blocks. Sometimes, when the wind's blowing in the right direction, we can hear an occasional roar.

Suzy thought I was ticked because we had to take Tyler along with us, and of course I was. I always am. But that wasn't the reason for my glumness.

It was a week after our visit to my grandparents, and the memory of what Mom had said just wouldn't go away. My mother is not the kind of person who talks just to hear her own sweet voice. She had given thought, I knew, to our moving out to Medsville. She had the house. The means and motive, as they say in mysteries. Now all she had to do was convince the jury: Dad, Tyler, and me. I wasn't going to give in. Not a chance. I didn't think Dad would either. At least, not easily.

Tyler would probably go along with the move idea if it meant he could have a dog. Mom kept saying we couldn't have one in the apartment.

"If we had a dog he'd protect me when I walked him late at night," my brother said. To which I replied, "You wouldn't have to be out late at night in the first place if you didn't have a dog!"

"Tyler!" I called out now as we came to the entrance of the zoo. "Don't rush off and get lost!"

"Oh, let him get lost," Suzy suggested. "That way you could be on TV, crying and saying, 'I just glanced away for a moment, and then my little brother was gone!'"

"I don't cry pretty," I said.

"Okay. Then you could cover your sobbing face, and *I* would face the cameras with a brave smile and say, 'My friend is inconsolable. She loved her little brother more than life itself. The rest of her sojourn here on earth will be pure misery if she doesn't get back the sib she so adores.'"

"That's not it either," I said. "Try, 'Her life will be living hell because of the flak she'll get from her mom.'" I didn't think my dad would be thrilled either if his son got lost among the wildlife. "Tyler!" I called. "Slow down!"

He stopped and as we came up, said in a high-pitched voice, "Tyler! Slow down!"

"And stop mimicking me! We're not home now, so I'm perfectly free to pulverize you."

"I want to see the apes," he said. "And don't say 'Just look in a mirror.'"

Suzy looked at me and shook her head. "Kids. You never know what cute things they'll come up with next."

It didn't hit the mark because Tyler had already run ahead to look at the signs with animals on them. "This way!" he yelled, trotting off toward the ape house.

We followed.

"Want to go in?" I asked Suzy.

"Are you kidding? With those smells?"

We sat on the rocky wall. The entrance and exit were right next to each other so there was no way we could lose Tyler.

"What's wrong?" Suzy asked me. "You've been gloomy ever since you came back from your grandparents' place. Are they sick or something?"

I broke down and told her what I'd overheard.

Suzy's mouth dropped open. "Are you *sure*? I can't believe your parents would actually do that to you."

"Mom would. I suppose she's suddenly decided the suburbs are best for raising kids. Or maybe she likes the idea of our grandparents being close by to help look after Tyler."

"You looked after yourself when you were his age," Suzy reminded me.

"I was a responsible child."

"What about your dad?"

"I don't think he'd like moving. But you know my mom. She can be a real bulldozer."

"Hmm." Suzy squinted her eyes, deep in thought. "We'll have to come up with good reasons for you not to move. Like . . . like . . ."

"I'd be totally miserable."

"That wouldn't cut it." Suzy knew my mom pretty well. "You could say it isn't fair to yank you out of school just when you're going into eighth grade. Everyone knows how hard it is to make new friends at our age."

"Right. Going into high school next year will be different. There'll be lots of new kids then," I added.

"So use the stalling technique," Suzy said. "Say they should wait a year so it would be easier for you to make the adjustment. American parents are always afraid of traumatizing their kids."

"Isn't your mom?"

"No. She's a little like my Grandma Lily. Do you know, Grandma asked me one day what *teens* are?"

"You're kidding!"

"I explained to her that they are the years from thirteen to nineteen when kids come into their own and start doing pretty much as they please. She said they never had such a thing in China. She said, 'Girls are little, then they are big. No teen do-as-you-want stuff.'"

"That sounds awful," I said. "Uh-oh. Here comes Tyler."

My brother came out holding his nose. "It stinks in there," he said. "I want to get something to eat."

"Why didn't you get one of your friends behind the bars to slip you a banana?" Suzy remarked.

Ignoring her, Tyler said, "I'm getting a Dove Bar." He ran on ahead and stopped at a cart peddling ice cream.

"We might as well all get one," I said to Suzy.

Eating the bars, we strolled along a path leading toward the pond. There was a line of people waiting to rent paddleboats.

"I want to go out on the lake," Tyler said. A big slab of chocolate fell off his bar into the dust.

"Don't you dare!" I warned, as he started to stoop for it. "And it's a pond, not a lake."

"Not a lake," he said automatically. And then, "I'm going. I have the money and I'm doing it."

"You can't paddle it all by yourself," I pointed out. "See, every boat has at least two people. Are you looking, Tyler?" I put my free hand on the top of his head and turned it toward the pond.

He squirmed away from my hold. "Okay. You guys can go with me."

"Forget it."

He gave the pond a sweeping look and said, "Then I'll find someone else to go with me."

"Sure you will," I said. "Come on."

Suzy and I strolled toward the big cat area, with Tyler lagging behind. The bars melted quickly in the heat of the afternoon, and between lifting off the chocolate sides and licking the ice cream, we were a mess. Fortunately we soon came to a water fountain. We stuck our hands beneath the stream to get off the goop. "Tyler, come on," I called over my shoulder as I gave my face a swipe. Then I looked. He wasn't there.

"Tyler!" There were quite a few people around, mostly mothers pushing strollers, with kids swooping around them. "Tyler!" I couldn't see him anywhere. "He's probably hiding behind a tree, just to yank our chains," I said.

Suzy was looking around too. "Maybe he went to see the polar bears over there."

We hurried to the enclosure and pushed our way through the three-deep ring of people, all straining against the railing to see the furry swimmers. No Tyler.

"Maybe he's at the back," Suzy said.

We raced around and down an incline which put us at water level. Standing at the windows, people could watch the bears swim, surface, and dive.

Again, we got rude looks as we pushed through the crowd of viewers at the windows. No Tyler there either.

Suzy and I looked at each other, both of us seriously worried now. I could see Tyler's picture on a milk carton: *Have you seen this child?* As unlikely as it seemed, kids like my brother did get stolen.

"We'll just have to keep looking," I said. "If I could only read his mind and know where he most wanted to go . . ."

Together Suzy and I exclaimed, "The paddleboat pond!"

We raced back and, panting, searched through the people standing in line. My brother wasn't among them.

"What'll we do now?" Suzy asked. "Should we try to find a cop?"

I felt sick. This was more than annoyance now—it was cold fear. Fear of what might have happened to my brother, and, I have to admit, fear of what would happen to me when I told my folks he was missing.

"Let's look just a little bit more," I pleaded. "He has to be around here somewhere. And if we do see a cop—"

"Maybe he's actually on the pond, in a paddleboat," Suzy broke in. "He could have talked someone into letting him join them. You know your brother."

That was certainly a possibility. I shaded my eyes and focused on the various boats. Some were quite near; others were at a distance, moving around a small island. "I don't see him."

"Wait—isn't that Tyler? Out there, by the big willow on the bank?"

"No, he wasn't wearing a red T-shirt." I began

checking out the boats coming around the island. "I still don't see him. Let's watch for five minutes, and then . . ." I hated to think of *then.*

Suzy, who had wandered to a higher bit of ground, suddenly shouted, "There he is!"

I looked to where she was pointing. Sure enough, there was my brother, coming down a park footpath. In the distance, behind him, I saw some guy hurrying away.

Tyler broke into a trot when he saw us. "Hey, where were you two?"

"Don't give me that!" I shouted, grabbing him by the shoulder. "Where were *you* and what were you doing?"

Tyler checked Suzy's expression and decided there was no help there. "Just talking to Paul," he said lamely.

"Paul! Who's Paul?" But before my brother had a chance to answer, I suddenly knew. "You were talking to that guy who's been shadowing Suzy!"

"Yeah. He's nice."

"*Nice!*" I screamed. "What are you, some kind of moron?"

Suzy was more interested than alarmed. "Did he tell you why he's been tailing me?"

"Naw. We didn't talk about you. He said I seemed like a nice kid and he'd like to get to know me."

"Flattery," Suzy observed. "To get information. Are you sure you didn't tell him anything about me?

You didn't give him my phone number or anything?"

"No. How dumb do you think I am? He said he might call me, though."

"You didn't!" I screeched. "You didn't give him *our* phone number, did you?"

Tyler shrugged. "I had to. It's unlisted, you know."

I was shocked into silence. Suzy and I stared at each other.

"Tyler," Suzy said finally, "you are such a loose cannon."

"Leave me alone," my brother replied. "I didn't do anything." He started stomping off toward home.

As we followed, Suzy asked, "Are you going to tell your folks?"

"If I do, you know whose fault it'll be."

"Sure. Yours, for not keeping an eagle eye on him."

"Right. But if I don't, and they find out . . ."

"Just be sure they don't. Threaten Tyler with instant annihilation if he blabs. That's always good."

"Hmm. Tyler!" I called.

"What?" He kept walking.

"Wait up. I have something to tell you."

Reluctantly, he slowed down. "What?" he repeated as I came alongside him.

"The folks are going to be furious when they hear

how you ran away and talked to a strange guy in the park," I said.

He looked at me. "Don't tell them."

"I've got to tell them."

"No you don't."

Suzy, who had come up beside me, said, "Too bad, Tyler. You'll never be allowed to go anywhere with us again."

"Don't tell!" my brother now pleaded.

"Gee," I said. "I don't know. What do you think, Suzy?"

"Give the kid a break. Don't tell," she answered. "But what'll you say, Ty, if this guy . . . this Paul . . . calls you on the phone?"

"I'll tell him 'wrong number!'"

"Good thinking," Suzy said. "Sometimes you're so smart."

We exchanged looks as Tyler skipped on ahead.

"I rather wish he had given the guy my number," said Suzy. "I'd like to ask him what's the big idea. Who is he, what does he want?"

"When and if this Paul guy calls," I told her, "Tyler could give him your number. Think you could handle it?"

"Sure I could. Only . . ."

"Only what?"

"What if . . ." Suzy stared at me and drew a deep breath. "What if it's really *you* that he's been shadowing?"

"Me?" I stood stock still. "Why would he be following *me*?"

"I've no idea." Suzy flipped back her hair. "Just a thought. Is there some deep, dark secret in your background?"

"Of course not. Unless you count a few uncles and cousins who happen to be vampires."

"We all have relatives like that," Suzy said. "But it could turn out that this Paul guy is just some ordinary creep with an ordinary mission, like wanting to sell your folks or mine an insurance policy."

"Suzy, I really don't think so."

"All right. But you know what I mean. He's probably following for some reason that's just as dumb. I wish it could be something sinister and spine tingling. This summer has been so dull."

I knew Suzy was just talking. She'd take off like a comet at the first real hint of danger. As for me, why waste time wondering? Either we'd find out who this Paul was, or he'd just fade. I hoped, though, that if he did call, I'd be the one to answer the phone.

CHAPTER 5

Mom was in the living room, talking on the cordless, when Tyler and I walked in. My heart gave a lurch. What did that guy do, head for the nearest pay phone?

But wait. There was something guilty in Mom's manner as she smiled brightly at us, then said into the phone, "Look, I have company. I'll have to talk to you later."

Company. "Who was that?" I asked when she hung up.

"No one you know. So?" With a return of the bright smile, "How was your trip to the zoo?"

This manner was not typical of my mother. Usually she zoomed in on us like a prosecuting attorney, asking for details. And she'd learned from all that courtroom exposure how to tell when someone was holding back vital info.

"It was okay," Tyler said. "I'm going to watch TV."

"I'm going to Suzy's," I announced, geared for the usual "But you just left her." This time it didn't come. I caught Mom glancing back at the phone as I left.

Suzy answered my usual knock-three-times knock.

"So?"

"Mum seems to be the word. Actually, my mom was on the phone, talking about that house, I'll bet. She made an excuse and hung up when we came in. How's everything here?"

"In an uproar. Grandma Lily is composing a letter. She says she may even turn it into a telegram. The worst has happened. Brandy has just run off with Brad."

"No!"

"And just when Brad's wife is about to deliver triplets."

"What a scum! Who's the telegram for?"

"Grandma wants to let Jessica know what's going on, and where the two of them are headed. Too bad we don't have e-mail."

"Who's Jessica, again?"

"Brad's wife, sieve brain. Don't you remember?"

"Oh, yeah. But didn't she just have a chin implant?"

"No. That's Charmaine, from 'Love Is an Oyster.' I don't see why you can't keep them straight," Suzy said. We walked over to the kitchen table. "How's it going, Grandma?"

"Too many words. Costs too much. Here, you fix it." She shoved the paper toward us as we settled into chairs across from her.

"It's written with Chinese characters," I murmured to Suzy, staring at the page. "Lots of them. Can you read it?"

Suzy kicked me under the table. "Course not," she barely muttered. Then, in a normal voice, she said, "Grandma, why don't you sleep on this? Or better yet, wait until tomorrow's show. Maybe Brad will come to his senses."

"Okay. We will wait. You hungry?" She always asked that. Most of the time we were, but not today.

"Grandma, no," Suzy said as the old woman bustled to the stove and began stirring something in a pot. "We ate at the zoo."

"Zoo?" She turned, ladle in hand. "What kind of food did you eat at zoo?"

"Ice cream."

"No good. Better eat some soup." She reached for a couple of bowls.

"Not now, Grandma." Suzy got up and motioned to me. I followed her to her room.

On her desk was a framed photograph, a duplicate of one on my chest of drawers. It was of Suzy and me, taken a year or so ago. As a lark one day, her mother had sat Suzy and me back to back on the floor, and divided our long hair down the middle and braided each side of it together—Suzy's long hair, black and shiny as licorice, and my long caramel-colored hair.

"It's so cute!" Suzy's mother had said, laughing, "the two colors intermingled. Look at yourselves."

We couldn't. We couldn't turn our heads or even shift our eyes back enough. Even standing up was impossible without help, joined at the scalp as we were.

"Here." Suzy's mom brought over a mirror. We could see the braids, but not distinctly.

"I'll take your picture!" She took several. In a couple we were clowning around with weird looks on our faces, but one was really good. That was the enlargement I was looking at now, an exact copy of mine.

"Look at us, so young," Suzy said with a mock sigh. "That was before you went ape over Mark."

"That creep. He's not even near being cute." I flopped on her bed. "But what about you and Jeremy?"

"He hates me."

"Sure he does. That's why he's always calling you up."

"For math answers."

"In the middle of the summer?"

Suzy just laughed.

I admit I felt a little twinge. Guys were always hitting on Suzy, and I knew that before long she'd start going out on dates. I mean, that's nature. You can have close girl friends, but sooner or later guys come along. But would they for me? Or would I just have to be content with accounts of Suzy's dates?

We heard her mother come in the front door and then go into the kitchen to talk to Suzy's grandmother.

"Mom?" Suzy left her room, and I followed.

"Hello there." Mrs. Wing said, turning to us. She kissed Suzy on the forehead and then me. "How are my girls?"

"Great. We went to the zoo this afternoon. Tyler got lost."

"Oh, no!" Mrs. Wing frowned with concern as we followed her into the living room. "Surely not for good?" Mrs. Wing's slight frown did nothing to erase her prettiness. Her complexion is perfect, and she has great cheekbones. She looks a lot like one of the beautiful Chinese actresses in the films she rents for her mother.

"Tyler was just goofing off," Suzy said.

I held my breath, wondering if she'd go on and tell her mom about the guy—Paul. Suzy told a lot more stuff than I did, but then her mother wasn't as paranoid as mine. Today, though, Suzy must have known that this was one of the things her mother would feel she had to discuss with mine. Although the two women weren't really close, they did compare notes now and then.

"I need you girls' opinions," Mrs. Wing said, opening her purse and taking out a long circular bundle wrapped in tissue. She laid it on the coffee table and opened it to reveal several bead necklaces.

"Cool beyond!" Suzy exclaimed, holding up a string of red beads interspersed with little golden Chinese symbols. "For me?" She always said that.

I opted for a seed pearl strand with coral accents. "Nice."

"They were shipped to us as samples from Beijing. Think we should order a bunch?"

"Sure," Suzy said. "I'd buy them in a minute. If I were older and wore stuff like this."

"I thought I'd take them along tonight. Check them out with the *older* ladies."

"Am I going along?" Suzy asked.

"Of course. Your aunts complain that you never go out to Chinatown, and there are some friends who want to see you too."

"Can Alexis come along?"

"No," I said. "I can't." I thought fast. "We're probably going out to dinner ourselves." This was a fabrication, but, I thought, a necessary one. My mother had always had this thing about my spending so much time at Suzy's, and lately it was getting worse. Sometimes I suspected she was jealous of my good relationship with Suzy's family. If so, it was Mom's fault. She never included my friend in our own family outings unless I made it an issue.

When we'd first moved in, Mom thought it was great that I'd made a friend so fast. But as time went on, she began hinting that I should make other friends as well. Once—and I'll never forgive her for this—she invited three girls over for a surprise birthday party, but not Suzy.

I was furious and hurt, but instead of confronting Mom, I sulked and ruined the party for everyone.

I knew Dad was angry at Mom, too, because I overheard them arguing about it. At one point Mom said, "Of course you'd take the Asian girl's side. Under the circumstances, that doesn't surprise me at all." I didn't hear any more after that but I always wondered exactly what she meant.

I knew that my father had worked in Hong Kong before I was born and had really liked it over there. He probably wished he could go back. Half the time when he came home and saw Suzy with me he'd say, "Well Suzy, been to Hong Kong lately?"

"Noooo," she'd reply.

She'd been there two years ago with her mother, but Dad always pretended she went regularly.

"You two, you've both been to Hong Kong, and I never have," I complained the last time he brought it up. "It's not fair."

Dad put his hand to his chest in mock horror. "Thirteen years old and never been to Hong Kong! What a disgrace."

"Easy for you to say, since you've been there."

"Yes, sweetheart, but I was in my late twenties and was sent there by my office. That's quite different."

Suzy asked, "Was Alexis' mom there too?"

"No. We weren't married then."

Dad left, and I said, "He worked for an electronics firm, but then they had him come back to the States. I wish he'd stayed, and I'd been born there."

"I don't think so," Suzy said. "If that had happened, you'd be someone else."

"I would? Who?"

"Ohhhh . . . someone cute." Suzy flinched, as if I were about to hit her. But I didn't.

❧❧❧❧❧

At dinner that night Tyler tried out another of his dumb trick questions.

"How far can a dog run into the woods?" he asked.

Dad really looked puzzled. "How far? I don't get it."

"Give up?"

"I give up."

"Halfway! The rest of the time he's running *out* of the woods!" Tyler said, gloating. "Get it now, Dad?"

I groaned. "That is so stupid, Tyler."

He ignored me and turned to Mom. "I'd like to have a dog."

No kidding, I thought.

"If we moved to the suburbs, I could have a dog."

There was general silence during which I held my breath. Then Dad said, "Well, we're not moving."

More silence, then Mom cleared her throat. "I have an announcement."

I stopped breathing altogether.

"There's a big case coming up next week, and they say it'll run at least three weeks."

"You're covering it?" asked Dad. Mom could more or less choose when she wanted to work.

"They asked, and I said I thought I could." She glanced around. "Any objections?"

I wondered why there'd be any objections and then I found out why.

"It would mean, Alexis, that you'd have to look after Tyler every day," Mom explained.

"Every day! Forget it!"

"Well, you can't go off and leave him here alone."

Tyler gave me a little smirk that made me want to smack him. "It's not fair!" I protested. "There are only a couple more weeks of vacation before school starts!"

"All right, forget it if it's too much of a hardship," Mom said. "I thought we could use the extra money, but then maybe you really don't want to continue ballet lessons."

"Come on, Lorraine," Dad said.

"All those extras add up," said Mom. "But that's all right."

I knew where this was headed: sailboat expenses, theater tickets, and so on. Mom always said we could afford these frills only because we had two incomes. I guess she was right, but did she have to throw it in our faces?

Once before, when Mom had complained about work, Dad had told her in that case to give it up; we could manage on his salary. Then Mom had claimed that he wanted to keep her chained to the kitchen (right!) and that he resented her having money of her own.

It was clear that Mom wanted it both ways. She wanted both the freedom to work and the freedom to bitch about it.

I glanced at Dad, caught in the middle as always, and then mumbled to Mom, "Okay, I'll baby-sit." Tyler, who preferred *child-sit,* glared. "We'll just go to the lake every day, that's all."

"Not the lake," Mom said. "Not until Tyler really learns to swim."

"What about the zoo?" I asked.

"The zoo's fine," Mom said, beaming at her little darling. "That's a perfectly safe place to spend afternoons. And it's a good way to learn about nature and animals."

I thought, *Yes, the two-legged kind.* What would happen if we ran into Paul again? What would we learn from him?

The thought of actually confronting the guy

made me feel a little shivery. But in the daylight, in a public place with Suzy and Tyler beside me, what could happen? Nothing bad, not if we were careful.

And I had to admit I *was* curious.

CHAPTER 6

The very next day, after Dad had left for the office, Mom announced that she was taking the next couple of days off, before the big trial commenced the following week.

"I'm going to run out to Medsville," she informed us, putting a cup of water into the microwave for her tea. "So you two get your stuff together."

"I'm not going," I said, rinsing out my cereal bowl.

"Excuse me?" said Mom.

"We were just out there," I complained. I put the bowl into the dishwasher.

"I know we were just out there. And we're going again."

"What for?"

"I'll drop you and Corliss off at the mall. You can look around for school clothes."

"I don't like shopping with Corliss," I told her.

"All right." Mom got a tea bag out of a jar and slammed down the glass top. It's a wonder it didn't break. "Don't shop for new clothes then. But don't expect me to drag you to Bloomingdale's later on, because I won't have time."

"I'll go with Corliss," Tyler-the-wimp stated. "I love the mall. Especially the pet store."

Mom, dunking the tea bag up and down, smiled. "You really do want a dog, don't you, honey?"

"It's my fondest dream," said Tyler.

I felt like making barfing sounds, but I simply told him, "Dad says you can't. You know you'd never crawl out of your little Mickey Mouse sheets on cold mornings to walk a dog. And don't think I would."

"Stop it right there," warned Mom as Tyler opened his mouth to yell. "You two just get ready."

Once in a very great while I can defy my mother and get away with it. I knew from her expression now that this was not one of those times. If I refused to go, she'd fly into a fury that would leave fallout for days to come. It wasn't worth it.

At least, I thought as I went to my room and exchanged my oversized night T-shirt for a daytime version, I'd get some new clothes out of the trip. I wouldn't check the price tags either!

I called Suzy and told her I couldn't see her that day.

"How come you're going out there again so soon?"

"Why do you think? For Mom to check out that lousy house is what *I* think."

"Tell her you've heard it's haunted. It gives off evil psychic vibrations."

"Yeah, sure. Mom believes only in evil people. It comes with her job. Besides, I may go to the mall and bankrupt us. Then we won't be able to move."

"That's the spirit," Suzy said. "Buy things I can borrow."

Before we left, I told Mom I'd decided to go shopping with my cousin after all. I knew Mom was really up to something when she willingly handed over her charge cards and said I could buy anything within reason. "If there's a problem, just have the clerk call your grandmother."

"Where will you be?"

"I'm not sure. But I'll be back to pick you up at Lord and Taylor's around three." She handed over some cash. "You can take Corliss to lunch."

When we got to Medsville, she left Tyler with Grandma Greta, dropped my cousin and me at the mall, and took off.

As I followed Corliss into the huge building, I thought I'd see if she knew anything. "I wonder why Mom wanted to come out here again so soon," I murmured. "Do you happen to know what she's going to do all day?"

"Who cares? Oh, let's go into the Gap. They have some dreamy tops. Are you allowed to buy anything?"

"Anything I want."

Corliss stared, blue-lined eyes wide, mascara-laden lashes aflutter. "Well! Let's get movin' here!"

I had to admit that without a parent to call time out, and with a cousin who majored in consumerism, shopping was not too shabby an experience.

"Should we be getting so much stuff?" I finally asked after a couple of hours had passed and we'd done major damage.

"Look, if your mom didn't give you a limit, how are you supposed to know how much is too much?"

"Okay." It certainly was a rare chance to go overboard. I'd even bought a red top that fought with my hair but promised to be a great bargaining agent when Suzy and I traded tops. Our two distinct colorings kept us from switching most of our clothes.

When Mom picked us up, she looked a little startled at all our shopping bags, but she laughed it off with, "Did you leave anything in the stores for anyone else?"

"You're so nice, Aunt Lorraine," Corliss said, sucking up. "My mom is going to throw a fit about just the few things I bought."

Because you probably do this all the time, I thought.

"Did you have a good day, the kind with the cute little smiley face and all?" Corliss asked my mom next.

Mom gave her a look, but said only, "Very good. I got a lot of things straightened out." Mom didn't explain, and my cousin, who had probably used up her being-polite-to-adults quota for the day, let it drop.

What did you get straightened out? The words were in my throat, but I couldn't say them.

On the drive back to the city, Mom slipped a tape of a book Tyler loved into the player. It kept him from fidgeting during the reverse rush hour traffic, and I guess it spared Mom from any questions about what exactly she'd been up to.

If I'd hoped to get the skinny from Dad's innocent questions at the dinner table, it was a lost hope. He had to work late and phoned to say we should eat without him.

I went out to the living room to greet him later that night, but he didn't talk much. Just kissed me on the forehead, glanced at Mom, who was reading a magazine, and went to his room. They'd been fighting again, obviously, but when? Mom might have called him at his office, from Medsville. If so, I wondered if it was about the house.

Last night Dad had said very definitely that we weren't moving. It would be just like my mother to have called him at the office today to say something opposite, like, "It's ridiculous to pay rent on an apartment in the city when I have this house in the suburbs."

Dad had asked Mom a number of times not to hassle him when he was at work trying to be creative. She did it all the time, though, because I guess she knew he wasn't as likely to yell and carry on if there were other people around.

I hated it when they were cool to each other at home. It chilled my heart. Tyler rather liked it, being the selfish little twit that he is, because Mom always paid a lot of attention to him when she was feuding with Dad.

❦❦❦❦❦

Suzy loved my haul of new clothes, which she checked out in my room the next day.

"It must be nice to have parents who let you buy stuff when they're mad at each other," she said, admiring the red top. "Why couldn't my dad show up now and then and make my mom miserable?"

"Would you know him if he did show up?" I asked.

"Probably not. I was just a baby when he took off. Could I try on these jeans?"

"Go ahead."

Suzy kicked off her Nikes, pulled off her shorts, and wriggled into the jeans. "I almost went to the zoo yesterday. To see if that guy Paul was hanging around."

"Why didn't you?"

"I was a little scared." She zipped up and looked at herself in the mirror. "You know, I thought of something. What if my dad hired him to kidnap me, like in that TV special we saw?"

"Those were little kids they kidnapped. If your father wanted you to live with him, wouldn't he just call and make all kinds of promises?"

"I guess. He won't, though. He's remarried, and I don't think his new wife likes kids." Suzy pulled off the jeans. "These are really cool. Would you mind if I got the same kind?"

"No. Go ahead. Do you ever . . . miss him?"

"Hmmm?" Suzy put her clothes back on. "My father? Why would I miss him? He's not a part of my life."

"I'd miss my father if he weren't around."

"That couldn't happen. Could it?"

I forced a little laugh. "Of course not, stupid." I leaped up and started putting the new clothes away. *People who argue a lot usually don't divorce because they air out their problems.* I could swear I'd heard that or read it somewhere. This fuss between Mom and Dad would blow over like all the others had. And the idea of moving to the suburbs would become history.

"Hello . . . hello . . ."

I turned around to Suzy. "What?"

"I asked you—" Suzy gave a little sigh—"if you'd heard from Paul."

57

"Who?"

"*Paul*! What's with you, Alexis? The guy I mentioned a minute ago. The guy who's been shadowing us. Am I getting through here?"

"I have a lot on my mind, Suzy. To answer your question, if Paul called, I didn't hear about it." After failing to yank a price tag from a top, I finally found a pair of scissors and cut it off. "It's kind of strange, isn't it? He follows us around, gets information from my brother, but then doesn't follow through."

"Right." Suzy sat on the bed and picked at a cuticle. "Nothing he does makes any sense."

"Maybe it does to him." I closed the drawer. "Maybe he has his own agenda."

"Oh, well." Suzy flipped back her hair. "We'll either find out who he is, or we won't."

We launched into a conversation about school opening soon and kids we knew, but only the top part of my mind could concentrate on what we were saying. Underneath, I had a doomsday kind of feeling.

It's nothing, I tried to tell myself. *Tonight everything will be fine. Just like the other times. Listen to what Suzy's saying. Lose yourself in the conversation. Lighten up!*

To my immense surprise, at dinner that night everything did seem fine. I realized my parents must have made up. They were actually talking to each other instead of directing all their comments to Tyler or me. Tyler looked a little miffed at not still being the center of attention, but I was glad things were back to the way they were supposed to be.

What caused this fight? I wanted to ask. *Was it about moving to the suburbs? If so, what have you two decided?*

I didn't bring up the subject, though. I wanted everything to continue to be quiet and relaxed. But inside, I knew this wasn't the end of it. Sooner or later the fights would erupt again. They always did.

CHAPTER 7

Of course Suzy and I didn't take Tyler to the zoo every day. Give me a break. We'd have gotten sick of seeing the animals, and they'd probably have felt the same way about us.

Several times we went to Water Tower Place, a mostly perpendicular mall on Michigan Avenue that has glass elevators and a waterfall. After we got tired of scoping out the shops, we'd go across the street to the big toy store and play with the computer games. Sometimes we'd just hang around Pearson Avenue and pet the horses that pulled carriages. There was a bus there, too, made up to look like a trolley. You could buy a ticket, stop off at any museum you liked, and then catch the next trolley. We did that twice.

All of this touristy stuff was okay for a while, but Suzy and I got tired of it. Finally one day, when the three of us were just hanging out, halfway ready to go somewhere, I said to Tyler, "Wouldn't you like to take a break and watch soaps with Grandma Lily today?"

He looked as though I'd offered him a summer sleigh ride. *"Could I?"*

I was a little stunned. "You'd rather do that?"

"Of course! What do you think!" He spun around and was gone in a flash, like Santa and his reindeer.

Suzy shook her head. "Kids. Go figure. Try to entertain them!"

"We'd better go down to your place and see if it's okay with your grandmother."

"Are you kidding? You know she's crazy about Boy Ty."

It was true. When he was little, she called him Baby Ty. When he was old enough to object, she switched to Boy Ty. They loved nothing better than to watch the soaps together, then carry on long discussions about them.

When we walked into the apartment, Ty was already perched beside Lily on the sofa, his eyes blinking at the carryings-on.

"What's that?" I asked, staring at the screen.

"'Itching Hives,'" Ty said.

The real name of the program was "Bewitching Lives" but we never called it that.

"I mean, what are they *doing*?" I kept staring at the screen.

"Getting ready to do brain surgery on Angelica. Ssshhh!" Tyler flapped his hand to silence me.

"That doesn't look like a doctor," I commented.

"It is not a doctor," Lily explained. "It is a bad biker with many kinds of clothing, all leather."

Frowning, Suzy asked, "But why is he pretending to be a doctor?"

Tyler gave a huge sigh. "Lily just told me it's because of that sauna at Thorny Rose's place and what happened in it. Would you two please shut up now?"

I turned to Suzy. "Want to watch?"

"At a time like this, how could we not?"

❦❦❦❦❦

It was the second week that Mom had worked steadily in court. The case was about a drive-by shooting, and, surprisingly, there were lots of witnesses. As court reporter, Mom had to take down everything anyone said on her steno machine.

At the slow rate the case was going, Mom said it might not wind up when they'd thought it would. There were lots of arguments between the lawyers, and they kept calling back witnesses.

This was not good news for me. Even though Tyler spent a lot of time with Lily, I was technically still in charge of him. I always checked to be sure he went there.

"Want to go for a walk?" I asked Suzy as we drifted toward her room on one of the days Ty was visiting Lily.

"Walk? What are you saying? Elderly people go for walks. I am in the first blush of youth. I do not go for walks."

"Please forgive me. Want to jog?"

"Can't. I've got cramps."

I heaved a sigh.

"Want to do something nice for your poor suffering friend?" Suzy asked.

"No."

"Go down to that new place on North Avenue and get some strawberry frozen yogurt," she said.

"No."

"Please? I saw some cute guys in there a day or so ago."

"Cute guys don't interest me. Especially the ones you think are cute, who look like road kills."

"Grandma Lily will pay." Suzy headed for the living room.

She came back with several crumpled bills. The old lady carried around serious money in her various pockets and readily parted with it. She used to press bills into her Boy Ty's hands every time he left—until I told the folks, and they made him return it. He'd stashed away more than twenty-five dollars and was furious at me for ratting on him.

"Okay, I'll go," I said as Suzy shoved the bills at me. "But only to get away from you."

"If you'd rather not get strawberry, choose whatever you want. I'm so easy to please. But try to make it strawberry."

Her high laughter went with me. Suzy was the most easygoing person I'd ever met. She was always so *happy*. She even sang while she was cleaning her room.

There was a short line at the frozen yogurt shop. I looked over the list of flavors and almost asked for mocha when I reached the counter, but what point would I be making? Everyone liked strawberry.

I was just going out the door when a voice said, "Alexis?"

Even before I turned, a little alarm sounded in my brain. Then I looked around and felt like a cat with its fur standing on end. It was the guy. Paul.

I couldn't speak.

"You *are* Alexis, aren't you?" His smile was gentle. His eyes, slightly slanted, had a tender look. I wasn't afraid, just immobilized.

"Wh-what do you want?" I finally managed to mumble.

"I'd . . . I'd really like to talk. Do you have time?"

"No!" And then, stupidly, I added, "The frozen yogurt will melt."

"Oh." His eyes didn't leave my face. He was quite a bit taller than I was. His hair, straight and parted so that the longer length dipped towards his left eye, was as licorice black as Suzy's. I guessed he was about eighteen.

I took a couple of steps, then stopped and looked back. He was standing there like a lost puppy. Was he any kind of threat? I didn't think so.

64

Surprising myself, I moved back toward him. "Why are you following Suzy?" I asked.

"Suzy?"

"My friend, the Asian girl. You know you've been following her!"

"Oh, the one who's always with you. No, you're mistaken. I've been following you and Tyler."

My heart gave a *thurump* like a baseball hitting a glove. "Why?"

"It's complicated. I can't explain out here on the street."

"Who *are* you?"

Again, the sweet, sad smile. "That, too, is complicated."

I didn't know where to take it from there. "I can't talk now. But you could call me. I guess." What could be the harm in that? "You have our phone number? Tyler gave it to you?"

"Yes. When would be a good time? When you're alone?"

That *alone* word was something I didn't like. On the defensive again, I said, "I really don't know. I've got to go now. Goodbye."

"Goodbye, Alexis. You're incredible. This whole thing is incredible." He looked at me as though he were memorizing—or remembering. But how could he be? I'd never met him before, I knew that. And still there was something. . . .

"Bye," I repeated, and walked quickly toward

home. When I turned the corner, two blocks farther on, I glanced back. He was nowhere in sight.

I hurried to Suzy's apartment and gave the knock.

"You'll never guess what!" I exclaimed when she opened the door.

"They had a 2-for-1 special?" She eyed the bag.

"I met—"

Tyler spotted me from the living room. "It took long enough!" He scrambled off the sofa and followed us to the kitchen. "Talia's locked in a cabin, and there are wolves circling. Derek's looking for her, but he just fell off his skis and broke his leg."

"Huh? What happened with the brain surgery?"

Tyler looked annoyed. "That's over. We're watching 'Love Is an Oyster' now."

"Good. Go back and watch."

"Commercial's on. Did you get any sprinkles for the top of the ice cream?"

"No, I didn't, and it's frozen yogurt." I took the two bowls Suzy had filled so far and pushed them at my brother. "Go."

"What's up?" His little face was deceptive. It looked so innocent, but a demon lurked inside. "Why do you guys want to get rid of me?"

Suzy said, "We always want to get rid of you, Tyler."

"Oh."

He was considering the truth of that when a shout came from his sidekick, Lily. "It's starting again, Boy Ty!" That sent him scurrying to the sofa, bowls in hand.

Suzy and I took the yogurt she'd dished up for us to her room and locked the door.

"Give!"

"I actually talked to the guy!"

Suzy looked perplexed.

"Paul!"

"You didn't!" Suzy's mouth opened wide in astonishment. "You actually talked to him?" Her voice rose higher and higher. "Just now? What did he say?"

"Uh . . ." What had he said, exactly? "He said he'd like to talk to me. Oh, and that he'd call. Oh, he also said I was incredible."

"Incredible? What's that supposed to mean?"

"No idea. He . . . Suzy . . . it was strange. I felt a little bit nervous, you know, talking to him. And yet in a way, it seemed almost natural."

"Don't forget we've spotted him a lot. So you've no idea what he wants to talk about? Or why?" She paused and took another spoonful of yogurt. "Did he ask about me?"

"All he said was you weren't the one."

Suzy laughed. "I'm offended. When's he going to call?"

Tyler pounded on the door. "Open up! Vice squad!"

"Oh, man." I got up and yanked open the door. "What do you want now?"

"I want some respect. And more yogurt."

"Go help yourself," Suzy said.

"I can't. I don't live here."

"Count your blessings," I said to Suzy as the three of us trailed back to the kitchen.

"Your blessings," Tyler repeated. I ignored him.

As Suzy plopped more frozen yogurt into his bowl, her grandmother called out, "Boy Ty! Come back fast. Wolves just broke in!"

Tyler left, saying, "I know you girls have a secret, and you'd better tell me, or else!"

I just gave him a bored look, and he left. As Suzy licked the spoon and then put the carton into the refrigerator, I complained, "Why couldn't I have had an older brother instead of that insect? Someone who could drive me places?"

"At least you're not an only child," Suzy said.

"I'm going home. He may be trying to call me."

"Who? Oh. We're back to Paul again."

We both went up to my apartment. The machine was blinking but whoever had called hadn't left a message.

❧❧❧❧❧

That night the phone rang twice, but when Mom answered there was no one on the line.

"It must be someone checking to see if we're home," she said.

"Or it could be someone connected with the case," Dad said. "Wanting to get to you."

"That doesn't make sense," Mom said. "If they wanted to talk to me, why would they hang up when I answer?"

I felt a prickling sensation at the back of my neck. Paul. I wondered if it was Paul, wanting to talk to me. Alone.

As if reading my thoughts, Tyler blurted out, "I'll bet it was that guy." He clapped his hand over his mouth, gave me a swift glance and then looked away.

Mom pounced, of course. "What guy, Tyler?"

"Uhhhhh . . ."

My heart started a staccato beat. I held my breath.

"What guy?" Mom repeated.

"Some guy who wants to give me a dog." My brother is almost brilliant at times. He'll probably be a lawyer some day.

"No dog," Dad said. "You gave this kid our number?"

"Yeah."

"Well, don't give our number to just anyone," Mom said. Tyler threw me a smug look.

That was the end of that, and I could start breathing again. One of these days it would probably come out. But I was glad it hadn't now. First I needed to find out more.

The next morning Dad left while Mom was still puttering around in her housecoat. "What are your plans for today?" she asked me.

I had almost forgotten. "I have ballet class. And I don't see why I have to drag Tyler along!"

"Okay. I'll take him with me."

I blinked. "To court?"

Mom was at the sink rinsing dishes, so I couldn't see her face when she said, "As a matter of fact, court's not in session today. So—" She stooped to put the bowls in the dishwasher. "I thought I'd run out to Medsville. Tyler can come along."

"You were just there."

"Is it against the law to go again?" She tried to sound light, but I could detect a strain in her voice.

"What for?" I persisted.

"Alexis." She slammed the dishwasher door, and I heard a spoon or something go *ping*. "I don't believe I have to account for my every move. Tyler, go get dressed."

Tyler dragged his foot back and forth on the tiled floor. "Maybe I don't want to go either."

"You don't understand!" Mom shouted. "I am not asking you, I am telling you. Now go!"

Tyler, giving a pathetic little sob, left.

"And Alexis," she said as she sponged off the table, "you can spend some time cleaning out your closet. Your clothes are jammed in there every which way, and it's a disgrace, all that stuff on the floor."

When I didn't say anything, she added, "Go through your clothes and put the things you've outgrown on a pile for Goodwill. That will at least make more room in the closet."

She went off to get dressed. Why hadn't she said anything about going to Medsville while Dad was still here? I thought I knew. She planned to settle everything and *then* tell him. But would Dad give in? Once again I could see a battle shaping up.

I was in my room, pulling out clothes and throwing them on the bed, when Mom paused in the doorway. She was wearing jeans and a top, which explained why she had stalled getting ready until after Dad left. She knew he'd ask why she was dressed that way when she always wore suits to work.

"Good, you've started," she said, looking at the pile of clothes.

When I didn't answer, she went on, "Why don't you ask Suzy to come help? It's always more fun to do things with someone else."

Were my ears deceiving me? Of course I'd intended to call Suzy anyway the minute Mom left.

"Okay, I will."

Tyler came along, and Mom started to leave with him. Then she paused. "Whatever happened with that stalking business? Does Suzy still think she's being followed?"

"No," I said. "She was wrong."

"That's good. You never know, in the city, what crazy things can happen."

"Yeah," Tyler piped up. "Or in the suburbs either. Remember that guy who went into the fast food place and shot up—"

"Let's go," interrupted Mom. "Be sure to lock the door if you leave the apartment, Alexis."

Later, Suzy sat on my bed cross-legged and put thumbs up or thumbs down as I held up clothes for her inspection.

"I didn't know you hated so many of my clothes," I said, as the pile of rejects grew. "It's not like you to hold back."

The phone rang out in the kitchen. We looked at each other and together said, "Paul!"

"Answer it, answer it, before he chickens and hangs up!" Suzy exclaimed.

I did. It was Dad, wanting to speak to Mom.

"She's not here," I said.

"I called the court and tried to leave a message, but they told me it's not in session today. Do you know where she went?"

"Uh . . . to Medsville. She took Tyler."

"Oh." His voice sounded strained. "Okay, thanks, Alexis." He hung up.

I made a grimace. "He's mad, Suzy. Mom didn't tell him she was going, and I guess he knows she's up to no good."

"The house?"

I pushed aside a bunch of clothes and flopped onto the bed. "Yeah. I'm really scared now. She's on a mission."

"Your dad doesn't want to move, does he?"

"Why would he? He loves the city as much as I do."

"Well . . ." Suzy pulled at a strand of her dark hair. "Then maybe you won't. Who's the boss? When push comes to shove?"

"I don't know." It was so hard to figure out my parents. When they had different viewpoints, sometimes Mom gave in and sometimes Dad did. If it was something like where to go on vacation, we'd all talk it over and come to a compromise.

But how could we compromise on where we should live? Mom—and Tyler, too, because of the dog—would vote for Medsville. Dad and I, for the city. There was no middle ground in this issue.

❧❧❧❧❧

It wasn't until later, when we were walking home from ballet class, that Suzy and I thought again about Paul.

"I don't see him around anywhere," Suzy said, looking up and down the street. "Maybe all he wanted was to see you up close and talk to you."

"What would be the point of that?"

"Maybe he's an artist, and you're his dream model. Now that he's memorized your face, he doesn't need to see you anymore."

"I'm sure." As a matter of fact I wasn't much interested in the mystery guy at this point. I was too concerned about what was going on at home. If Mom thought—if she actually thought—! Tears spilled from my eyes.

"What's the matter?" Suzy asked. "Why are you crying?"

"I'm not crying."

Suzy understood. Softly, she said, "We won't let it happen. We just won't."

"I know." Of course I didn't know at all. But just for the moment, it felt good to pretend that Suzy and I could keep things just as they were.

CHAPTER 8

Mom and Tyler came in at about five, carrying groceries. Mom was still putting things away when Dad walked in, surprising all of us.

"Harvey, you're early," Mom called out. "What's up?"

"That's what I'd like to know," Dad said, pitching his briefcase onto the sofa near me and striding toward the open kitchen.

"What do you mean?" Mom asked.

"You know very well what I mean. You were out there again today."

I glanced nervously around to see if Tyler had gone to his room and stayed there. He had. In a way, I also wanted to leave, but in another way, I didn't.

"So what if I did go out there? Is there a law against it?" Mom slammed the refrigerator door so hard that a couple of Tyler's drawings, along with the magnets holding them, fell to the floor. "Do you have a problem about my driving to Medsville?"

"You know what the problem is." Dad was standing by the open counter between the kitchen and living room. "You're up to something, and I'd like you to tell me exactly what."

"I've tried to tell you," Mom said, her voice rising as it always did when she was on the defensive. "But you just won't discuss it like a reasonable human being."

"There's nothing to discuss! We're not moving out there, and that's all there is to it!"

"You're not the only one to be considered. How about what *I* want? You never think of *my* feelings!"

"We made a decision to live here," Dad said. "And now we're staying. I'm not putting this co-op on the market. And I'm not leaving!"

"All right, stay. But if I decide to do it, I'm taking the kids and moving to Medsville whether you come along or not."

"We'll see about that!" Dad shouted.

He turned and noticed me in the corner of the room, taking it all in. I'm sure my face was white with shock. He hesitated, came to me, kissed the top of my head, and picked up his briefcase.

"Dad . . ."

"I'll talk to you later, sweetheart." He gave Mom a quick look and headed for the front door.

"Where are you going?" Mom started out of the kitchen, but Dad just walked out.

As the door slammed, Mom gave me a look that was part surprise, part fear. I jumped up and ran to my room. *I hate all this!* I was thinking. *And I hate what Mom's doing to our family.*

I sat on the edge of my bed feeling so bleak I couldn't even cry. It felt like a heavy weight was on my shoulders.

After a while I heard Tyler go down the hall. His voice and Mom's came to me as sounds, not words. After a few minutes my brother rapped on my door and told me dinner was ready.

"Dad had to go back to the office," he explained as I eyed the three places set at the table. "When I grow up I don't want to work in advertising," he said. "I want to be a poet, like Grandpa, and grow vegetables to eke out a living."

Eke. Where did he get that word? One of these days I was going to explain to Tyler that Grandpa, before he retired, was editor of a travel magazine. Right now, though, I was too depressed to say anything.

Mom had heated up some leftover spaghetti and made a salad. Tyler was the only one with an appetite. I couldn't get anything past the stiffness in my throat, and Mom just picked at her food.

After a few bites, she got up. "I'm going to my room," she said. "I have a headache. You two can clear up when you've finished."

I just sat there, staring at nothing. The minute she left I got up and carried my dishes to the kitchen. I scraped the food down the disposal.

"You shouldn't waste food," Tyler said. "Think of all the hungry children—"

"Oh, be quiet," I muttered.

I waited for him to finish, then cleared his plate. I thought about going down to Suzy's but I didn't want to face Suzy's mother. She's so sensitive she'd know by looking at me that something was wrong. I didn't want to discuss it.

Tyler hung around forlornly, waiting for me to finish in the kitchen. As I turned out the light, he said, "Alexis, would you read to me? I'm feeling very blue."

He could read very well for his age, but he looked so sad and appealing that I agreed to read from a book that was a little beyond his own skills.

We sat together on the sofa and I thought Tyler was caught up in the story, until he put his hand on my wrist.

"What?" I asked, stopping.

"When is Daddy coming back?"

"I don't know."

"I think I'll go ask Mother." He started to slide off the sofa, but I stopped him.

"She has a headache, remember? So don't bother her—she's probably asleep. Why don't you go to bed too?"

With a little whimper in his voice, Tyler said, "But who will tuck me in?"

Oh, really! I knew he was playing for sympathy,

but since I really did feel sorry for him, I agreed to tuck him in.

I was off to bed myself after that, but I had a hard time falling asleep. Where was Dad? What if he never came back? What would happen to us?

❧❧❧❧❧

The next morning I was still only half awake when Mom opened my door and said, "Get up, Alexis."

As I turned my head on the pillow to look at her, I heard Tyler stamping and shouting, "I don't want to go there again today!"

"Tyler." Mom's voice was unusually calm. "Remember what we talked about yesterday? Our secret? Well, just think of that and stop this nonsense."

Still sleepy, I staggered out to the kitchen. "Has Dad already gone?"

Mom hesitated and then said, "He's not here."

He hadn't come home!

"I'm not in the mood for any nonsense out of either of you," Mom said, pouring milk on Tyler's cereal. "I have to go out to Medsville to make some decisions about my house, and I want you both along. Is that clear?"

I shrugged. "Can Suzy come with us?"

It was automatic to ask this, and the answer was

usually, "Not this time." So I was quite surprised when Mom said, "I don't see why not."

I realized later that Suzy was to play the role of buffer, to keep me from asking questions Mom wasn't ready to answer.

Suzy, assuming we were going out to see my grandparents, was delighted. She was crazy about them, and they thought she was a great kid.

While Tyler and I were in the hall, waiting for Suzy, I asked what the secret was between him and Mom.

"You're nuts if you think I'm telling."

"Does this little secret go 'arf arf'?"

My brother is so transparent. I knew I'd hit the mark by the way his eyes widened behind his rimmed glasses and his mouth dropped open. Then came his usual intelligent response of making a fist and hitting me on the upper arm.

Bribery. My own mother was using bribery. That hurt worse than the punch he'd given me.

We started off in the car with Tyler sitting beside Mom, as usual, and Suzy and me in back. It was a beautiful sunny August day, but my soul felt black.

This is it, I thought. This is the beginning of what my future is going to be—a move to Medsville. Didn't Mom realize that moving out there would ruin my life? I guess not. And I couldn't tell her.

Mom and I never had easy conversations the way

Suzy and her mother did. I was always hesitant to speak my mind because basically I was afraid of Mom, afraid of how she'd react. And so I just kept quiet.

After the toll road zapped us past the last city buildings, we came to a stretch of scenery.

"Just look at those fields of wheat," Mom said.

"I think they're soybeans," Tyler corrected.

"Whatever. It's so nice to breathe the fresh air of the country."

I was surprised my brother didn't point out that we were breathing air-conditioning in the closed-up car.

Suzy, sounding like the voice of innocence, said, "Mrs. Dawson, would you ever think of moving back out this way?"

I felt like kicking her ankle, but at the same time I was very curious to see how Mom would answer.

She met Suzy's look in the rearview mirror and said, "Well, that's an idea, Suzy. Wouldn't it be nice if we did? Then you could come out for a whole weekend visit."

"Yes, that would be nice," Suzy politely agreed.

I suspected Suzy was thinking the same thing I was. What was a weekend now and then, compared with seeing each other every day? If my family lived in Medsville, there would be thirty miles separating us. We would no longer be sharing school events and classmates, and, impossible as it seemed, in time we'd surely drift apart. The very thought of it gave me chills.

We stopped off at my grandparents' house.

The first thing Tyler said was, "Grandpa, I'm going to get a dog!" What a great keeper of secrets he was.

"You're really getting one?" Grandpa asked.

"Well," Mom said, trying to cover up, "It's just something we talked about. It's not for sure."

Before Tyler could work up into full-blown indignation, Grandpa suggested they go outside to see the new birdbath. "It's in the shape of a cat, lying on its back, paws holding the bowl. Hope it doesn't confuse the birds."

"Put up a sign," Tyler said as they went out. "Say 'Just kidding. The cat is not real.'"

"Suzy," Grandma Greta said, "it's wonderful to see you again. You get taller and prettier all the time. And so does Alexis here. Do you girls have a secret for staying the same height, no matter how much you each grow?"

"It's just concentration," Suzy said, smiling.

"Well, you're lucky to have each other."

Mom, who was looking a bit uncomfortable, said, "Is it okay if I leave Tyler here? The girls can come along with me."

"Where to?" I asked.

"To the house I inherited. Do you remember going there to visit your other grandparents?"

"Yes."

Suzy frowned. "Isn't that where you used to live, Alexis?"

"No. Dad and Mom and I lived in Winterlake. It's not too far."

"When I was a girl, I lived with my parents in the house I now own," Mom explained to Suzy. "That's how I met Alexis' father. He was raised here, right in this house. We met in high school."

I wondered how long we were going to drift down memory lane.

"Let's go, girls," Mom said. "We won't be long. I just want to make some decisions about decorating. The rooms need painting, and I may have one of the bathrooms redone."

"Come back for lunch," Grandma Greta said.

"Oh, no, we can't, but thanks." Mom fished the car keys out of her purse. "I've got to go down to the court this afternoon and check out my notes. The case begins again tomorrow for sure."

The house was about a mile away. It was a small white colonial, with pillars on the front porch. Mom parked on the circular driveway and got out of the car.

Suzy scuttled out, too, and waited for me. I guess she could tell I wasn't eager to enter this house, sitting there as if it were ready to swallow up my life.

We followed Mom inside. She took a memo book out of her purse and began making notes. Suzy and I wandered around.

"It has a real dining room," Suzy observed.

"So?"

"And the kitchen's big." As I remained silent, she added, "What I'm saying is, it's not bad. If you want to live in the suburbs."

"Which I don't."

We went upstairs. There were three bedrooms and two baths.

"It's nice and roomy," Suzy commented.

"Would you please stop trying to make me feel good?" I said, irritated. "I wouldn't want to live here even if it had an indoor pool."

As we were going downstairs, we heard voices.

"Oh, girls," Mom exclaimed as we joined her, "this is Mrs. Warshaw from across the street, and her daughter, Beverly. You girls are all the same age. Isn't that marvelous?"

I felt like saying, "Why?" but instead grudgingly said, "Hi. I'm Alexis, and this is Suzy."

Mrs. Warshaw, a woman with short, cropped hair and a figure that looked like the cover of an exercise video, said, "Why don't you all run across the street and get acquainted?"

Again I felt like saying, "Why?" but shrugged instead.

"Come along, then," Beverly said to me. She looked like a sample size version of her mother, except that her hair was a little longer.

"Come on, Suzy," I said as she stood, uncertain.

"Oh, yeah, she can come along too," Beverly said.

As we followed her across the street, she said, "My friends call me Buffy."

Suzy gave me a sidelong look but didn't say anything.

Beverly (I knew I would never call her Buffy) led us through a one-story ranch house and back to her room.

"Mom says you live in the city," she said to me, ignoring Suzy altogether. "How can you stand it? All that dirt and noise!"

"You go there a lot?" I asked, checking out the various trolls lined up along a shelf. The shelf had a polka-dot ruffle along the edge and the bedspread was polka-dot too. The rug was an ugly shade of green with a purple pattern on it.

"Me, go to Chicago?" Beverly gave me a strange look. "Why would I want to do that?"

"To visit museums, see plays, the ballet."

"You've got to be kidding. People out here don't do that stuff. We don't have time, for one thing."

"Oh, really?" I asked sweetly. "So what do you do instead?"

"We go to games, school dances. And hang out at the mall."

"The mall," I said. "Heavy stuff."

"I spend a lot of time with my computer too," Beverly said. She whisked a polka-dotted cover off the machine, which was sitting on a desk. "I want a laser printer, though, instead of my dot matrix."

"But it goes so well with all the other dots," Suzy murmured.

Beverly, after a quick glance, decided to ignore that. Turning back to me, she asked what kind of computer I had.

"None. But my dad lets me use his sometimes."

"What does he do?"

"My dad? He's copy chief at an ad agency." As Beverly just looked at me, saying nothing, I went on, "He plans and sometimes writes copy for advertising campaigns."

"He's very smart," Suzy volunteered.

Beverly didn't even look at her. "I suppose he makes a lot of money."

"Well . . ." I felt uncomfortable with this conversation. "I think we ought to go back, Suzy. Mom said she didn't plan to stay long."

"Okay. Nice to meet you, Barfie," Suzy said.

Beverly glared. *"Buffy."*

"Bye," I said. The laugh I was holding back erupted as Suzy and I crossed the street. "Suzy, you're awful," I said. "Wish I'd thought of it. Barfie is the word for her, all right."

Suzy said, "After that she'll never be friendly to me. But then she never would have been anyway. I hope I didn't ruin it for you, though, Alexis."

"Huh. She'd never be a friend of mine, even if I lived across the street from her. Which I never intend to do."

"Yeah," Suzy said, but I could tell there was a doubt in her mind. We smiled at Mrs. Warshaw, who was coming back across the street, but didn't say anything.

Mom, alone now, was holding different paint swatches against the living room wall. "What do you think of this one, girls?" she asked, checking out a pale salmon color.

Since I refused to answer, Suzy said, "It's nice."

Just then Grandma Greta drove up with Tyler, who ran into the room where we were, ahead of her.

"Lorraine," Grandma said, "Harvey just called. He asked me to tell you that he's going out of town."

"He is?" Mom looked really surprised.

"To Minneapolis, for a meeting. It must have been sudden."

"Maybe, maybe not." Mom looked at us. "Kids, go out to the car. I'll be right along."

I heard Grandma say, as we were leaving, "Lorraine, I don't want to butt into your affairs, but it worries me, the way you two seem at odds. Can't you get together on this house situation?"

"When I try to talk to him, he just gets angry," Mom said.

Suzy and Tyler had already gone outside, but I lingered at the door, trying to hear more.

"Harvey's always had a temper," Grandma Greta agreed. "But Lorraine, you've got to win him over with reason. If you can."

"If I can," Mom said. "If I can't . . ."

Just then Tyler yelled at me to come outside. I had to, or Mom would have known I was listening.

"If I can't . . ." What then, I wondered. Who would win the argument, Mom or Dad? And in the knock-down, drag-out fight that followed, who would be hurt?

Tyler and me. It was always that way. The kids were always the losers.

CHAPTER 9

There was no message from Dad on the machine when we got home. Mom had no idea how long he'd be in Minneapolis.

"Let's just go out and eat," she said. "I'm a little tired."

"It's a long drive from Medsville," I said. And thought, *How would you like to do it every day you had a court case?*

"What if Dad calls?" Tyler asked. "And he needs to talk to us?"

"He'll just have to call back, won't he?" Mom picked up her purse. "Let's go, kids."

We walked over to Wells Street where there was an outdoor restaurant. The tables were white metal with yellow umbrellas propped over them.

The waiter, a young blond man with a gold hoop in one ear, took our orders. He called Tyler *sir*, which seemed to amuse Mom, but annoyed me. Tyler already has an inflated opinion of himself.

With Dad so noticeably missing, it was hard to have any kind of normal conversation. Besides, there were all those secrets we were keeping: Mom, with her somewhat hidden plans for a big family move; Tyler with his poorly kept secret of the dog he planned to get; and me with the secret knowledge of Paul.

"Both of you," Tyler said, "I'll bet you can't say *fish* with your mouth closed."

Mom pulled her thoughts from wherever they'd been and looked at Tyler. "Fiii . . ." she tried. "No, you can't say it with your mouth closed."

Tyler, delighted, looked at me. I knew it was a trick question. He'd actually asked if you could say the sentence *Fish with your mouth closed,* rather than the word *fish.* I decided to let him have his little triumph. "Fiii . . . No, it can't be done."

With a whoop of joy, my brother said, "'Fish with your mouth closed!' Get it?"

"That's a really good one," I said. "Have you tried it out on Grandpa?"

"Not yet. When are we going out again, Mom?"

"I'm not sure. I have to be in court now for a while. The case is starting up again."

"Maybe Dad can take me out."

"Maybe." Mom's glance caught mine for just an instant before she looked away.

I had the feeling that she was concerned and a little scared about Dad taking off without talking to her. And then it occurred to me, *Maybe he didn't go*

*out of town at all. Maybe it was just an excuse to
stay away from us.*

"Want to go to a movie?" Mom asked, with little
enthusiasm.

"No," Tyler said. "We've already seen all the good
children's movies. Why can't we see the others?"

"In your case, I don't know why not," I said.
"You've already seen all there is to see on the soaps."

❦❦❦❦❦

The next morning, almost as if he knew it was
safe, Paul called a half hour after Mom left for work.
"Could we meet somewhere and talk?" he asked.

"What about?"

He laughed. "Many things."

I felt too flustered to make a decision. "I'm kind
of busy right now," I said. Well, I was. Busy putting
red polish on my toenails. "Could you call back in a
while?"

He agreed, and I immediately phoned Suzy. "Paul
wants me to meet him! Eeeeeeh! What should I do?"

"Go for it. But make him meet you somewhere
out in the open."

"Okay. Want to come along?"

"If I did, he might just fade away, never to return."

"I doubt that, Suzy."

"I know! Meet him at a bench in Lincoln Park. I'll

sit on one opposite, across the wide walk. In disguise, like a celebrity."

"Which bench? There are dozens over there."

"How about across from Dearborn Street? Lots of people walk by, so you could yell out if Paul got sinister. Not that he looks the type, but you never know."

"Okay, I'll call you back and let you know what time."

❧❧❧❧❧

I was decidedly shaky some time later as I walked to the park, as planned, for the meeting. Tyler had gone down to Lily's to check out what was happening on the brain surgery front.

I saw Paul waiting at the appointed bench. Then I looked over and saw that my bodyguard was indeed on duty. Suzy had gotten herself up in a floppy hat, sunglasses, one of her mother's dresses, and her ankle strap shoes. I think the effect was supposed to be glamorous. As I watched, she took a copy of *Vanity Fair* from a big, floppy purse.

Paul said, "I'm so glad we could meet. Want to walk?"

I could just see Suzy trying to tail us, wobbling all over the place in those high heels.

"Let's sit here. I can't stay long," I told him. "What did you want to talk about?"

"Everything. Anything. To begin, I should tell you

something about myself. I live in San Francisco."

For a crazy second I felt like someone on the show "Most Wanted," and wondered why I was being tracked down. Then I asked, "What are you doing here?"

"I'm about to register at the University of Chicago. You know of it?"

"Sure. It's out by the Museum of Science and Industry. Smart kids go there."

Paul smiled. "To the university or the museum?"

"Both, I guess."

He cleared his throat. "At present I'm staying with a friend of mine on Wentworth Avenue. In Chinatown."

"Oh?"

Paul's looks and voice were so gentle I really couldn't be afraid of him. "My mother," he said, "is Chinese. My father is not."

I decided to cut to the chase, as they say in movies, even if my question seemed blunt. "Paul, why did you want to meet me?"

"So I could get to know you."

"But why? Why me?"

"I wish I could tell you. I will, soon. I know it's asking a lot, Alexis, for you to trust me."

"I guess it is, and I probably shouldn't, but I do." I shrugged and gave a little laugh. "Trust you, I mean." Was it intuition that told me Paul was not a threat? "What do you want to know?" In spite of my trusting him, if he asked something like *Are you often alone in the house, and when?* I was out of there!

His question, though, was safe enough. "What do you like to do when you're not in school or baby-sitting your brother?"

"Read. Bead-weave; I make little bracelets and belts and things from beads and thread or leather. And I go to ballet class too."

"You want to be a dancer?"

"Not really. But it's fun." I went on talking about ballet and *The Nutcracker* that Suzy and I danced in each year. Then I got onto things that happened at school. Before I knew it, quite a bit of time had passed, and I'd done all the talking.

"Alexis," Paul said, "I've really enjoyed meeting you like this. You're even more than I'd hoped for."

Seeing my puzzled frown, he said, "I know this must all be very strange and confusing to you. I wouldn't blame you if you raced home and told your parents we'd had this talk. But I truly hope you won't."

I didn't know what to say.

"It's just for a little while. As soon as possible, I'll tell you whatever I can. That is . . ." He raised his shoulders in a shrug. "If everything works out."

"Am I going to see you again?"

His smile quickened. "You're willing?"

"Yes, I guess so." Actually, I wasn't even ready to leave him now. "Will you call me?"

"Of course." He shook hands. "Thank you."

"Thank *you*." Why was I thanking him?

He smiled and released my hand. Then he glanced over at Suzy, smiled even more, and left.

I sat back down on the bench, wanting to think over the things we—or I, mostly—had said. I could almost still feel Paul's presence, but then Suzy came lurching across the walk on her high heels.

"Take those things off before you break something," I said.

She sat down, unbuckled the ankle straps, and got out of the shoes. She exchanged them for flip-flops that she pulled from the oversized bag. "Did he tell you anything? Why was he shadowing you?"

"I still don't know why." I repeated to Suzy what Paul had told me, which wasn't really much at all.

"I can't see why he'd want to listen while you babbled out your whole life story," Suzy said. "If you were the kid of someone famous, and he were a reporter, that would be different. But as it is, why should he care about you?"

"I don't get it either. I have the strangest feeling about him. It's as though I've always known him, but we've been separated and are just catching up."

"*He's* the one catching up," Suzy reminded me. "You still know zilch about him."

We started walking home, Suzy flip-flopping and no longer wearing the hat.

"Is he going to call you again?"

"He says he will. I wish I'd asked him for his number. All he said was he's staying in Chinatown temporarily."

"*Chinatown*? Totally cool," Suzy said. "Be sure to give me advance notice before you meet him next time so I can think of a different disguise."

"Lose the idea of disguise, Suzy. You didn't fool Paul today. I could tell by the smile he shot over at you."

"Really? What gave me away, I wonder?"

"I can't imagine."

"So why's he shadowing you?" Suzy shifted the bag to her other shoulder.

"We didn't get around to that."

"Oh, great job. Don't ever consider being a detective as a career choice."

When we entered Suzy's apartment, I walked over to where Tyler and Lily were watching the screen. "What's going on with 'Itching Hives'?"

"It is difficult to relate all that has happened," Lily answered.

"Alexis doesn't really care anyway," Tyler said.

True. I went to Suzy's room, where she was changing into shorts and top.

"I can't believe you didn't ask the vital question," Suzy said, pulling her long hair out from under the neckband. "He said he wanted to meet you, yes. But why?"

I dropped down onto her one easy chair and brought my knees up to my chin. "It's just one part of the mystery connected with him. The whole thing's like a box within a box."

"I hate mysteries."

"You do not," I told her. "What are you doing there, Suzy?" She was peering into the mirror and had scissors in her hand.

"I'm cutting a few strands."

"For bangs?"

"No, random lengths."

"Why?"

"To make me look exotic. It's an Asian thing. You wouldn't understand."

"Oh, I see." I took a few strands of my own hair and pulled them across under my nose. "Since when have you gone so Asian?"

"I don't know."

Mrs. Wing appeared in the doorway. "Hello, Alexis. What don't you know, Suzy?"

"I didn't know it was so late. Oh, well." Suzy put down the scissors and faced her mother. "What do you think?"

Mrs. Wing raised her eyebrows slightly. "If it pleases you." She paused. "In fact, I do like it." She gave Suzy a little hug, ran her hands over my hair, and left. She came right back. "Suzy, I almost forgot. Do you want to go with me to your aunts' house for the Moon Festival?"

"I might. When?"

"Next month, full moon. Alexis, you're welcome, too, of course." Her smile was sincere. I wondered sometimes if Suzy realized how lucky she was to have a mother who was so easy to be around. I suppose Mrs. Wing got angry occasionally, like anyone else, but those times must be rare. I'd never known her to be anything but cordial, and I saw her every day.

When she left, I asked Suzy, "What do you do at the Moon Festival? I forget."

"Just sit around and eat cake. Mooncake. In olden days the girls and guys used to sing and dance and carry on, even read love poems, but that would be a drag today." She looked at herself in the mirror and arranged one strand of hair in front of her right eye. "It'll be boring without you. Maybe even with you. Can you come?"

"What?" My mind had wandered. "Oh, to the Moon Festival. Maybe." I got up. "It depends on what else is going on."

I hadn't told Suzy about Dad leaving for Minneapolis, if that was where he'd really gone. Somehow I just couldn't talk about it. I still suspected he'd left just to get away from us.

❧❧❧❧❧

My suspicions grew stronger when Dad showed up not long after dinner. "Dad, you're back so soon?"

"It was a rush business deal." He put down his brief-case and an overnight bag I knew he kept at the office for just such sudden trips. "Where's your mother?"

"At her book review club."

"I thought she might be. Come and talk to me while I pack, Alexis." He moved down the hall, and I followed.

"Pack? Where are you going now?"

"I'm moving out for a while."

"Moving out! You don't mean that!" I sat on his bed and watched with horror as he took a suitcase from the back of the closet and began to put his underwear and socks and shirts into it. He pulled out a garment bag and hung several suits inside. It looked as if he planned to move out not for a while, but for a very long time.

"You're leaving for good!" I started to cry. "How can you do that? How can you leave me?"

"Honey, it's not you I'm leaving." Dad reached over and smoothed my hair. "I'll always be here for you."

"No, you won't! Fathers say that, and then they take off."

Dad sat next to me, but he didn't touch me. "It's not an easy decision, you know. Your mother and I both tried, but it's just not working out."

"It'll never work out if you leave!" I reached over to the bedside table for a couple of tissues and wiped my tears. "You'll just go away, and Mom will drag us out to the suburbs."

"She's going to do that anyway, whether I stay or leave."

"Why does she want to move? Why would she want to live out there and drive in to work?"

"Apparently she thinks living in the suburbs is worth it. I don't happen to agree."

"Can't you stop her, Dad?"

He sighed. "I don't see how. She's been at me to move for a couple of years. Now with her own house available, well . . ."

"It's a dumb reason for breaking up a family."

Dad got up and resumed packing. "There's a lot more, Alexis, that we don't need to go into."

"What? Why not? Tell me!"

Dad zipped up the garment bag. He was about to close his suitcase, but then he reached over to the bureau and picked up a framed photo of him and Tyler and me. His taking the picture made it all seem so final. I felt angry at him for this desertion and at the same time very, very sad.

He snapped the suitcase shut and picked up a pad of paper he kept on the bedside table to jot down advertising ideas. "If you can't reach me at the office, try this number." He wrote down a number and handed me the paper.

"Where is this?"

"A friend's apartment. He's going to Europe for a month or two, so I'm subletting."

"Take me with you!"

"Honey . . . honey, I can't do that."

I jumped up. "You don't want to! Neither one of you cares about *my* feelings!" I thought of something else. "What's Mom going to say when she comes home and finds you gone?"

"She knows I'm leaving. I called and told her so this afternoon."

My mouth dropped open. "And she went out anyway?"

Dad looked at me for a moment and then looked away. "It seems she did, Alexis."

I flung myself against him, sobbing. "Dad, Dad, don't leave us! I don't want to live here if you're not here!"

He held me, kissed the top of my head, and then pushed me gently away. "It will all work out somehow, Alexis," he said.

"How can it?" I sobbed even harder.

"I promise you I'll keep in touch. I'll take you out to dinner. You can spend the evening with me."

"Are you and Mom getting a divorce?" I reached for still another tissue. I couldn't stop crying.

"We haven't talked about a divorce."

"But does that mean you might?"

"Alexis, please don't make this any harder. We won't do anything to hurt you or Tyler if we can possibly help it." He kissed me, picked up his bags, and left.

I heard him talking briefly to Tyler out in the living room. Then I heard the door close.

My eyes were red and swollen. I didn't want to go

out and get Tyler upset. He must think Dad was just going out of town again. Let him think it. Mom could set him straight.

Mom! How could she go off to some stupid book review meeting when our life was falling apart? Didn't she care? Or didn't she want to face Dad? In a way, her being gone had avoided another big shouting match, but that didn't mean it was right. I might never forgive her for going off when she knew Dad was leaving.

I went to my room and sat in the dark, crying, remembering different things our family had done together. Mom and Dad had often disagreed and had had their famous shouting matches, but things had never before gotten to this stage. Now it seemed that there was no way to save our family. It was being ripped right down the middle.

Tyler knocked on my door. I let him in, but didn't turn on the light.

"Your voice sounds all foggy," he said.

"It's because I'm sad."

"Why are you sad, Alexis?" He rubbed my arm and leaned against me.

"Because . . ." I couldn't go on.

"Are you ever so blue and lonely?"

"I guess."

We both heard the front door open. Tyler darted from the room, and I closed the door and locked it.

I heard Mom coming down the hall and Tyler trailing after her.

His voice was higher than usual, almost squeaky. "I asked Daddy if he wanted to wait and tell you goodbye, but he said I could tell you for him. So goodbye from Daddy."

Goodbye from Daddy. Those were the saddest words I'd ever heard.

CHAPTER 10

I hadn't said good night to Mom and I wasn't about to say good morning either. I waited until I heard her leave before I went to the kitchen for breakfast.

Tyler, who'd already finished his cereal, looked pleased to see me. Without his glasses, his face had a very young, unfinished look. "What shall we do today, Alexis?"

I gave a little groan and thought, *Either he has no clue about why Dad left or he doesn't really care.* "I'll see," I said, thinking, *I'll go to my room, where Tyler can't hear, and I'll phone Suzy and tell her what happened last night.*

I jumped at the sudden ringing of the telephone. Tyler grabbed for it and turned to keep it out of my reach.

"Hey, Paul!" he said. "How are you? No, just Alexis and me." After a little more conversation, he handed over the receiver.

"I was hoping you two would be alone," Paul said. "I'm out near the university, just got my room. And the Museum of Science and Industry is so close. I wondered if it would be possible for you both to meet me there?" Apologetically he added, "I know this is short notice."

"I guess we could meet you." *Why not?* I thought. "What time?"

"Whenever you can make it."

We arranged to meet in an hour and a half, and I called Suzy. She could go, of course. I thought of leaving a message for Mom or Dad, but then I decided they could just worry. Maybe if they worried long enough, they'd break down and call each other.

I usually loved the ride along Lake Shore Drive on a sunny day like this, with sailboats skimming the blue waters of Lake Michigan or bobbing in the harbor. But today I kept thinking of all the happy times Dad had taken me sailing.

"You seem so sad," Suzy commented. "Is it about Paul?"

"No." I looked toward the front of the bus. Tyler, kneeling on one of the side seats and looking at the lake, couldn't hear. "It's Dad. He split last night."

"Split? You mean, for good?" There was shock on Suzy's face.

Tears came to my eyes. I swallowed. "I hope not. But he took lots of clothes. I'm so mad at Mom for doing this—for driving him away."

Suzy took hold of my wrist. "He'll come back. They'll work it out. They always do."

I nodded but didn't believe it.

We got to 57th Street and the museum a half hour early. I suggested to Suzy that she take Tyler, who was jiggling with impatience, inside to get a map of the museum exhibits. I'd sit on the wide steps outside and wait for Paul.

They took off, and I sat there. I tried to think of Paul, rather than the situation at home, but it was hard to do.

Paul came along just a few minutes later. Without my wanting to, I started to cry.

"Alexis! What's happened?" He took me by the shoulders and looked into my eyes. "What's wrong?"

"It's just . . . it's just . . ." I struggled to control my voice.

"Let's go sit on the steps over there, beyond that pillar."

He waited while I pulled myself together.

"It's my dad," I finally said. "He left us."

Paul's reaction was not what I expected. Instead of simply looking concerned, his face actually paled. "He left? Does it . . . does it have anything to do with me?"

"You? Why would it have anything to do with you? My folks don't know anything about you," I answered, wiping away tears.

"Are you sure?"

"Yes. I haven't told them. Neither has Tyler. If he had, I'd certainly have heard about it."

I looked at Paul, who was staring into the distance and biting his lips. Why was he so upset? "What's going on?" I asked. "I mean, what do you know about my parents?"

He took several deep breaths and then looked at me. Then he looked away again.

Was this weird, or what? "Paul," I finally said, "you've got to tell me. Do you know my parents?"

"In a sense," he said. "But not really."

"I don't think they've ever been to San Francisco, where you're from," I said, trying to understand.

"No. But your father's been to Hong Kong."

"A long time ago. So?"

"He knew my mother there."

I was too shocked to respond. I just stared at Paul.

"As you say, it was a long time ago." He twisted his fingers together.

"How did he meet her?"

"They worked for the same electronics firm. She translated Chinese into English or French and helped write instruction booklets."

"And they became friends? Your mother and my father?" This was certainly a strange thing to think about.

"Yes, they became very good friends." After a pause, Paul said, "Actually, they fell in love."

"In love!"

"It happens, you know. People working closely together . . ."

"But what about my mother?"

"Your parents weren't married yet. They'd known each other a long time, as I understand it. And had dated. But they'd split up when your dad was transferred to Hong Kong."

This was all so surprising I didn't know what to say.

Paul examined his nails. "I probably shouldn't be the one to tell you all this. . . ."

"Well, no one else has. What happened, Paul? Did the two of them get engaged?"

"More than that. They got married."

"Married!" A strange, tingling sensation went up my spine. "My father married your mother?"

"Yes. It was a Buddhist ceremony. They were going to get married again in your father's faith when they got back to the States."

"What do you mean, *were*? What happened?"

"My mother was called home to China because of the death of a relative. The Chinese political situation was very complicated then, Alexis. Once people went back to China they often had problems getting out again."

"Didn't my father go after her?"

"No, that was impossible."

"Well, did they at least write?" Perspiration was running down my back.

"If your father wrote, and I'm sure he did, she didn't get the letters. She thinks he didn't get hers either."

"Then what did they *do*?"

Paul shrugged. "They couldn't do anything. Your father was transferred back to the States. He never knew about me."

"You?"

"Yes. I was born in China."

My mouth fell open. I was practically in shock. "Are you saying . . . Are you saying my father is your father?"

"That's what I'm saying." He looked at me steadily. "So now do you see why I was so anxious to meet you? You and Tyler?"

"But—" And then it dawned. "Paul!" Now I started to tremble. "You're my *brother*?"

"Well, half brother." He looked away. "I hope you don't mind."

"Mind! Paul, this is so . . . so . . . I can't believe it!" I kept looking at him. It felt as if the world had fallen away around us, and we were all alone, sitting on the steps and gazing at one another.

"So there you are!" A voice broke into our reverie. It was Tyler. "What're you guys doing way over here?"

Then came Suzy, clattering down the steps in her cowboy boats, saying, "We glanced outside but didn't see you behind the pillar. Why are you just sitting there? Why didn't you come on in?"

Paul and I stood. I suddenly felt very shy and uncertain. How is a girl supposed to act, I wondered, when she's just found out she has a big brother?

"Alexis and I had things to talk about," Paul said.

Did we ever! I thought. I'd already decided I wasn't ready to share this great news with anyone— not even Suzy, and certainly not my brother. Not yet. I had to think about it. Mom, Dad, they had to know first. It was fantastic that I knew before either of them. My head buzzed.

"Paul, you've got to see the coal mine," Tyler said, taking his hand. *His brother's hand!*

"Sounds great." Paul and I exchanged a shared, secret kind of look, then he and Tyler trotted off, with Suzy and me following. *He has the same walk as my dad!* I thought. His smile, too, was a little—

"What's the matter with you?" Suzy asked, staring at me. "Have you taken a zombie pill?"

"I'm just . . ." What could I say?

"If it's about your parents, try to put it on hold. You can't do anything, at least not today."

I nodded. Actually I'd forgotten about them for the moment. But now a new rush of worry flooded me. What would happen when they found out about Paul? I didn't dare think about it.

Later, when we were standing in line outside the coal mine, I whispered to Paul, "Let's just keep this between us until we can decide what to do . . . how to break the news to my parents. It's really going to knock them out. I'm in shock myself."

"So am I, a little," Paul said. "I've dreamed of meeting my dad for years. But then, when it finally became possible, I felt panicky. That's why I looked you up first."

It didn't occur to me yet to wonder how he knew about me.

☙☙☙☙☙

There wasn't another chance for Paul and me to talk alone for the rest of our stay at the museum. Tyler clung to him like a leech, and Suzy was never far away.

When it was time to leave, Paul shook hands with Suzy and gave Tyler a mock punch on the shoulder. A long look passed between Paul and me as we, too, shook hands. "I'll call you very soon," he said. "If you can't talk, I'll understand and will keep on trying until it's safe."

"Nice guy," Suzy said as the three of us headed for the bus stop.

"The best," Tyler said. "I like him. I think he likes me too."

"I'm sure he does," I said. And then I went on to wonder how much Mom would like Paul, if at all. I knew Dad would *like* him well enough. But how would he feel about this total stranger of a son coming into our lives?

Walking along, I made a resolution. Even if my

parents didn't want to include Paul in our family, I did. All my life I'd wished for a big brother, someone I could confide in, who'd always be on my side. And now here he was. And he was perfect.

Paul, I said to myself, *it doesn't really matter what anyone else says or does. You and I are brother and sister. No one can change that.*

CHAPTER 11

That night at dinner I caught Mom staring at me a couple of times. I suppose she was surprised to find me in such a good mood all of a sudden.

"Well, I'm glad you had such a nice day," she remarked after Tyler described our trip down to the mine in boring detail. "But in the future, let me know when you plan an excursion."

"We decided to go after . . ." Tyler caught himself. I'd repeated to him over and over when we got home that he was not to mention Paul. ". . . after you left," Tyler said to Mom. The kid was really good at thinking fast to keep himself out of trouble. But instead of just letting it go at that, he went on. "It was so lonesome around here, with Dad gone." He even managed a little controlled sob.

Don't overdo it, I wanted to warn him, but his words had a good effect on Mom, who let him have a double dessert.

As we watched TV together later on, all three of us lined up on the sofa like the Brady Bunch, I saw the TV antics through a blur. Paul's face kept cropping up, smiling or looking sad. It seemed very strange to me that here I was, knowing all these startling things about our family, and neither Mom nor Tyler had the slightest clue.

Mom, I thought, *did Dad ever tell you he was married to someone before you?*

Later on, as I lay in bed, questions winged through my mind. How long had Paul known? How had he found us? Did Dad have even a hint that he had another son, and that son was right here in town? On and on the questions came, but of course there were no answers. I tried to quiet my mind by concentrating simply on the fact that I had a big brother. It would be so wonderful to get to know him.

But there was a down side too. When Mom found out, how angry, how hurt would she be? Would it be so bad that she'd yank Tyler and me to the suburbs for sure? Would she divorce Dad? Would she try to keep us kids from seeing our father?

I didn't think she would or could, but you never know.

❧❧❧❧

Suzy bopped down bright and early the next morning, animated as always. "Guess what Grandma Lily is getting."

"An operation?" Tyler said.

Suzy gave him the merest glance. "A fax machine."

"What?" I half-choked. "You're kidding. A *fax*?"

"Yesterday she went with Mom to her business place, for a change of scene. She was so impressed with the fax machine's coughing up reports that now she's buying one for herself."

"I don't get it. Why?" I asked.

"So she can fax letters to the stars of soaps, without any wait."

Tyler piped up. "Those machines must be expensive."

"Grandma has money. But what a waste!" Suzy rolled her eyes.

Tyler looked serious. "Not if it makes her happy."

Moments like that, seeing Tyler's innocent little face, made me believe there might be hope for my brother's growing up human. Or maybe it was just Lily. He was so devoted to her that anything she did was fine with him.

❦ ❦ ❦ ❦

Suzy, Tyler, and I went over to Lincoln Park later on, taking books, sandwiches, sodas, and a baseball and gloves. We played three-way catch for a while, then sat on benches and read and ate our lunch.

Suddenly, swallowing, I almost gagged. The

phone! The phone could be ringing, and I wasn't there!

If Paul called and there was no answer, would he assume I had decided I wanted no part of him? Would he give up or wait a long time to call again? I didn't even have his number.

Then I thought of something else. What if he left a message on the machine! I had to get back to listen and then erase it before Mom got home. You could never be sure about her hours. Sometimes court shut down early because the judge had other duties, or a juror got sick.

"I've got to go home!" I said.

Suzy looked at me curiously. "What's with you? Why are you so spacey?"

"Spacey?"

"Yes. First you act like someone in a seance, hearing voices from beyond. Then when I say something, you give a jerk, like you're coming back to the here and now." In true Suzy fashion, she put her hand against her chest and joked, "Oh, have you been possessed? Are there demons fighting to take control?"

"Something like that," I said carelessly, thinking, *Should I tell her? Do I dare?*

"I'd like to go home," Tyler said. "It's boring here. I want to visit Lily."

"That's right," I commented. "You missed 'Itching Hives' and all the rest yesterday. How did the brain surgery go?"

"They didn't operate. There was a big storm and

116

all the power went out just as the doctor was ready to drill."

When we got back to the apartment, I checked the machine. There were no messages. Tyler took off for Lily's.

I realized I couldn't go on pretending with Suzy, trying to act normal. She knew me too well. Sooner or later I'd have to tell her. I decided it might as well be now.

"Sit down, Suzy," I said. "Here on the sofa."

She shrugged. "Okay."

"I've got a secret. A really big secret."

"Like what?" She eyed me warily, concerned.

"Promise you won't tell."

"You know I won't. What?"

I paused, took a deep breath, and said, "Paul's my brother. My half brother."

Suzy's mouth dropped open. For the first time since I'd met her, she was speechless.

"Are you surprised?"

She continued to stare. Then she said, "Alexis? Are you just saying that about Paul because you *wish* it were true?"

"Of course not. He really is related. He told me yesterday, when we were sitting out on the museum steps."

Suzy shook her head as though trying to clear it. "But how could Paul be your brother? I mean, he's Asian, isn't he?"

"Partly. From his mother. My dad knew her when he worked in Hong Kong, years ago."

"And so?" Suzy looked absolutely baffled.

"Okay. I'll tell you everything I know, which isn't everything." I poured out what Paul had told me—was it only yesterday? Except for an occasional "No!" Suzy was stunned into silence.

When I finished, she began asking questions. "How come Paul told you first? How did he find you? What are you going to do next?"

"I don't know. I don't know. I don't know," I responded to all three.

"What about your mother?"

"Suzy, I don't even want to think about it. When she finds out!"

"Hope I'm not around. So. You're sure your dad doesn't know about Paul?"

"Absolutely. Dad wouldn't hide such a thing. You know him. You and I—and Paul, of course—are the only ones. I told you about it because I just had to tell someone."

"Wow." Suzy, who had been sitting cross-legged on the sofa, now crossed her arms as well. She leaned her head back so that she was gazing upward into space. "This is like something you'd see on TV."

"It's not a soap opera," I protested.

"In a way it is. You have this couple, your mom and dad, who date each other in high school. Later on your dad goes overseas, meets and falls in love with this beautiful woman. . . ."

"Did I say she was beautiful?"

Suzy waved away my objection. "They get separated, the man finally goes back home and marries his high school sweetheart. But then, wow! This son turns up! So it really is like a—"

"You can stop. You've made your point." I didn't like the idea of my parents' life, and Paul's, being treated like one of Lily's whacked-out soaps.

Suzy stared at me. "What happens next?"

"I guess you'll just have to tune in tomorrow and find out."

I said it lightly, but I really was concerned. All I could see at the moment was total wreckage.

We couldn't let our lives be ripped apart. Paul and I would have to figure out a way to break the news without breaking up the family. What would that way be? I hadn't a clue.

CHAPTER 12

I heard a key in the lock. I leaped from the sofa and then stood nervously, looking guilty as sin. As Suzy later observed, *If it had been your mother, she'd have had the story out of you in no time flat.*

It was only Tyler, looking upset and frailer than ever. Behind the horn rims his eyes were full of fear.

"What's the matter, Ty?" I hurried to him. "What's happened?" *Did it have something to do with Paul?*

Tyler took off his glasses and wiped tears from his eyes. "I'm just so scared. I didn't mean to say it. But—" He wiped his face again.

"What did you say?" I grabbed his arm. "Did you tell Lily about meeting Paul?"

"No." Tyler took his arm out of my grip. "It was worse than that."

Worse? How could it be worse? "Tell me exactly what you said!" I glanced at Suzy, who also looked concerned.

Tyler cleared his throat and put his glasses back

on. "I thought Lily would be happy for me, so I told her about the dog."

"What?"

"The dog I'm getting when we move to Medsville."

If we move to Medsville, you mean, flashed through my mind, but it wasn't the right time to say it. "So then what happened?" I asked.

"Lily got all funny looking. Her face squished up, and she started making funny sounds, and I got scared. I would have called 911, but I didn't know the number."

"That *is* . . . oh, never mind." Suzy was already headed for the door. Tyler and I followed.

As we raced down the stairs to the floor below, I was thinking, *Don't let her have had a heart attack, Don't let her be dead!*

We tore inside the apartment to find Lily hunched on the sofa—alive! "Boy Ty! Boy Ty will go away, leaving Lily," she wailed. "Lily will not see him again!"

"Oh, Grandma!" Suzy flopped beside her, and I sat on the sofa arm. Tyler stood in front of her, clenching and unclenching his hands.

"Lily," Suzy continued, "Tyler isn't going to leave you!"

"Yes, I am," Tyler said in a small voice.

I glared at him and mouthed the words, *Shut up!*

"It isn't for sure he's moving, is it, Alexis?" Suzy said.

"That's right," I said.

"But even if he should move . . ." Suzy paused while Lily let out a wail. "Even if he should, he'd come to see you often. Wouldn't you, Tyler?"

"Yes, I would, Lily," Tyler said, blinking back fresh tears.

I spoke up. "I'd come in to see Suzy all the time, and I'd bring Tyler along." This was no time to mention that I myself had no intention of moving.

Lily wrinkled her face at me. "You say you will, but you will forget."

"No! I'll never forget you or Suzy. You can count on that, Lily." I could hear in my voice the tone my own mother uses when she wants to get her point across.

"Words, words," the unconvinced woman said. "They sound good but mean nothing. When Boy Ty gets dog, he will forget Lily."

Suzy rolled her eyes in exasperation. Softly she said to me, "Let's just leave her alone. There's no use trying to talk to her when she's like this."

She got up, and Tyler took her place. He picked up the remote and turned on the TV. "It's time for 'World Beneath Blue Skies,' Lily. Let's see if they've found out which triplets are Jessica's." To me, he explained, "Someone switched all the babies in the nursery, and now she has two boys and one girl instead of two girls and one boy."

"Oh, honestly." I went out to the kitchen with

Suzy where we calmed our nerves with a diet drink.

"It would be so cruel if we had to move," I said. "It would ruin so many lives."

"Yeah. And the timing is so bad, too, what with Paul and everything." Suzy reached up into the cupboard and got a bag of fortune cookies from Chinatown. "Want one?"

"No, thanks," I said. "Those things taste like sweetened cardboard."

"Take it anyway." She shoved a cookie at me. "You never know; you might get some great advice." She broke her own apart and pulled out the tiny tissue. "Hey, get this: *True love is within your grasp.*"

"Maybe you're getting a dog too."

"Who do you think it really means? Matthew? Someone told me he likes me."

Irritably, I said, "Go on, believe it if you want to."

"Read yours."

I crumbled the cookie, took the paper and read to myself, *The things you wish for most you can achieve.* I showed it to Suzy. "Sure. I'll really put my trust in this."

"You know how to make it happen?" When I just stared at her, Suzy explained, "The Moon Festival is coming up soon. So what you do is, put the fortune on a saucer, burn it down to ashes, and then blow the ashes up toward the full moon. It works every time."

"Suzy, you are so full of it."

"Okay. Don't believe me. But I'm not going to fly in the face of fortune. This may be just what I need to get a romance going with Matthew. He's so cute and cool."

I crumpled up my paper fortune and was about to toss it, but then I thought, *What if Suzy's right?* So I stuck it into my pocket instead. At least it could give me some hope.

❧❧❧❧

The next day passed, and still there was no call from Paul. I was annoyed at myself for not asking for his number.

On Saturday Mom told Tyler and me that we were going to the suburbs.

"Suzy can come along," she said.

"I don't think she'll want to," I said. If Mom was trying to get on my good side, too bad. I wasn't that easy. "There's nothing to do out there."

"Excuse me," Mom said. "I was under the impression that you two just hung out together and talked. I didn't know you had these big social plans every day."

Now she was being sarcastic, and I hated that. "I'll ask her if she wants to go," I said, and I left for Suzy's.

Actually she couldn't go. She'd promised Grandma Lily that she'd take her to an electronics store to look at fax machines. "Tell you what, though," she said. "When we get back, I'll slip up to your place and check for phone messages. If Paul has called I'll take down the information and then erase."

"Great!" I left her my key and went back home.

Out in Medsville, I asked to be dropped off at Grandma Greta's. I wasn't going to show any interest at all in the house, but Tyler elected to go along with Mom. I think he wanted to nail down the dog deal.

I went out to the garden with my grandparents and helped them gather vegetables. The tomato vines were drooping with the late summer harvest.

"You take a bunch of these back with you," Grandpa said. "I don't know why I planted so many."

"I don't know either," Grandma said. "The freezer's already packed. And our neighbors have so many you can't even give them away. As for the zucchini, they've totally taken over the back lot."

She and I went into the house, and she found a bag for the vegetables I was to carry home.

Then we sat down at the kitchen table. "How are things going for you, Alexis?" Grandma Greta asked in her kind, husky voice.

I started to answer, but my throat clogged up.

"It's hard, I know. But sweetheart, you just have to hold on and trust that things will turn out all right. They usually do, you know. It may take a while, but . . ."

125

"I feel so bad about Dad."

"Of course you do. It's hard on everyone."

I tore at the edges of a paper napkin. "Are you mad at Mom?" Grandma had a right to be, driving her son out of the house.

"No, honey, I'm not mad at anyone. I just wish the situation could be resolved in such a way that everyone would be happy."

I wanted so much to tell my grandmother about Paul, but I didn't dare. I did begin, "When my father worked in Hong Kong—"

Her dark eyes darted at me. *She knew something!* "What about Hong Kong?" she asked carefully.

Oh, what could I say? "Did he tell you about his life there? About everything that was going on?"

Abruptly Grandma got up. "I think I'll see if I can find room in the refrigerator for the rest of the tomatoes." Then, her face hidden from me, she said, "Your father told us lots of things, but in letters you only say so much. And then, when he got back, I don't know . . ."

Did he tell them about the Chinese girl he married? I couldn't ask. There was no way I could mention that romance.

Just then Grandpa came in with still more vegetables, and the Hong Kong subject was dropped. I noticed, though, that despite Grandma's casual talk, she had a guarded look. She was probably wondering

why, out of nowhere, I had started talking about
Dad and his overseas job.

❦❦❦❦

When Mom and Tyler and I got home, I rang our
buzzer.

"What'd you do that for, stupid?" Tyler asked.

"Just checking the system," I lied. It was actually
a warning to Suzy to scram out of the apartment if
she was there.

I phoned her as soon as I could. "No calls," she said.

Darn! What was I supposed to do now? What
could I do? Nothing but wait.

"Grandma Lily and I looked at fax machines,"
Suzy said. "But she didn't buy one. I think the sales-
man thought she was a little twilight-zoned." She
laughed, then went on, "Just say yes or no. Has anything more happened between your parents?"

"No."

"Has anything more been said about your moving?"

"No."

"I wonder why you haven't heard from Paul."

"I wonder the same thing. Look, Suzy, I've got to
hang up. Talk to you later." I was afraid I'd say
something that might be overheard by either Mom
or Tyler.

When I went out to the kitchen, though, Mom

was there, checking out leftovers with little or no enthusiasm. Dad, she said, was coming by to take Tyler and me out. The news both pleased me and worried me a little. Of course I'd be glad to see my father, but would he be able to tell by looking at me that I knew something secret?

While Tyler and I were waiting for him, Mom seemed a little on edge. She tried to act nonchalant, but I noticed she had put on fresh makeup and had changed from jeans to a pretty summer dress.

Dad didn't even come upstairs, though. He rang from the lobby, and Tyler and I went down to meet him.

Neither Dad nor I wanted to go to the new chain restaurant down the street that Tyler wanted to try. We compromised on an Italian place that he didn't actively hate.

As my brother sucked up a soda he said he needed right away, Dad asked me how things were going.

"Okay," Tyler said, lifting his top lip from the straw. "Alexis?"

I shrugged. "Okay. It's lonesome, though, without you there."

Dad looked away. Silence. Then, "I guess school will be starting soon. Eager to go back?"

"Are you kidding?" Tyler said, and burped. "The only good thing is the dog I'm going to get. I'll be kind of scared, though, going to a new school."

"Dad," I pleaded, leaning toward him on the

table, "do we have to move to the suburbs? Can't you do anything? You're the *father*."

He sighed. "Eventually, I might be able to do something, Alexis."

"Can't you talk to Mom? I mean, do you guys hate each other so much you can't even talk? Even if it means saving my sanity?"

"We don't hate each other, your mother and I," Dad said. "We just . . ." He took a drink of water. "The timing, I know, is very bad, just now when school is about to begin. But I promise you, Alexis, I'll have a talk with your mother. See if we can work something out."

"You mean get back together?" Tyler asked.

"I mean about where you live, go to school."

"I need to go wash my hands," Tyler said, scooting out of the booth. He did this all the time, everywhere we went.

"You washed just before we left home," I reminded him.

"Yes, but I've touched things since. The doorknob, the table . . ."

"You're sick," I told him. As he trotted off I said, "I don't know what he'll do if he does get a dog. Carry around spray wash and paper towels?"

"He'll outgrow it. I notice he doesn't repeat your words any more." Dad smiled.

"That's right. You know, I hadn't noticed."

We were silent for a few moments. Then suddenly,

surprising even myself, I asked, "Did you ever want to go back to Hong Kong?"

"Hong Kong?" Dad looked startled. "Why do you ask?"

"Oh. . . ." I felt so wimpish. "Suzy often talks about going there. I'd like to go, too, some day." Then I added boldly, "I should think you'd want to see it again, meet up with old friends. . . ."

"I doubt that there's anyone I'd want to see all that much."

"You mean out of sight, out of mind?"

"No, Alexis, I mean that I've lost touch."

Tyler came back then. "I have to say the facilities are fine here," he announced. "Blow dryers instead of paper towels. Far more sanitary."

"You're beyond weird," I said.

"Beyond weird," he repeated.

Dad and I looked at each other and laughed. From then on the evening went pretty well. I was sorry to say goodnight to Dad. "Don't you want to come upstairs just for a while?"

"Not tonight. But I promise we'll all get together and talk," Dad said. "Very soon."

There wasn't a lot of time. I could see that moving van rolling up to our door, and me being dragged, screaming and kicking, out to Deadsville.

"Dad, make it very, very soon," I said. "Or I might do something desperate." *Like run away*, I thought.

Dad just put his hand over mine.

I would, I thought. *I could run away to Grandma's.* But then I realized that that didn't make any sense. Grandma herself lived in Deadsville, the very place I didn't want to be.

CHAPTER 13

It was the next afternoon, and Suzy and I were alone in our apartment, when the phone rang. I answered it on the first ring.

"Hi, Alexis. Can you talk?"

"Sure," I said, trying to keep the excitement out of my voice. "I've been waiting for you to phone." To Suzy, standing there, listening through every pore, I mouthed, "It's Paul."

"My life has been pretty hectic," he said, "signing up for classes, meeting people, and looking for a part-time job."

"I would have called you, but you didn't give me your number."

He paused, then said quietly, "There was a reason." Another pause, and he continued, "I'm very confused."

"You are? About what?" *Was there a mistake? Was I not his sister after all?*

"About this situation. The thing is, all I wanted at first was to see you and Tyler. But when I did, that wasn't enough. I had to meet you, talk to you, find out what you were like."

I felt a little stiffness in my middle. I forced myself to say, "We weren't what you, uh, expected? We disappointed you?"

"What? How can you even think that? You two are great! And that's the problem."

I pulled a stool up to the counter and sat. "What do you mean?"

"Now that I've found you and met you, I want you to be part of my life. And that's not good. It could cause a lot of discord."

"No!" Even as I said it, I knew he was right. It could cause major damage. "But Paul, it's done. We can't undo it now. We've met and we're family. I don't want to lose my big brother!"

"Alexis." His voice was a little strained. "I blame myself for all of this. I was selfish to want—"

"No! You weren't! You have a perfect right!"

"To barge into your life and your father's after all these years?"

"Yes. It would be a great waste for us not to know one another."

"I have no idea what your father's like, you know."

"My father? He's your father too. He's fun and fair and great to be around. You'll see."

"What about your mother?"

Yes, what about Mom? When she heard about Paul, she would freak out, to put it mildly. "Mom is . . . what can I say? A little more, uh, nervous than Dad."

I glanced at Suzy, who made a fanning motion with her fingers.

"But she'll just have to accept it," I went on. "We'll worry about that later. First you've got to meet Dad. You want to, don't you?"

"Of course, but I'm thinking about you. What it could do to your life. From what you've said, it's in a muddle already."

"True. But isn't it better for you to meet Dad face to face than to have Tyler blurt out your name and something about you, even if he doesn't know who you are? I'm amazed that he hasn't done it already."

"Actually, so am I. A kid that age—"

"So let's do it." My heart fluttered nervously at what my mouth was saying.

"Alexis, think it over. And I'll think it over. Let's not rush into this and be sorry afterward."

"Okay. Give me your number, and I'll call when I have a plan."

He did, and I wrote it down and stuffed the paper into my jeans pocket. We said goodbye and hung up.

Suzy, who had pulled up a stool, leaned her elbow on the counter and raised her eyebrows at me. "Can I be around to applaud when the fireworks start?"

"Oh, man, I'm scared. Suzy, what should I do? I'm too young to have this much responsibility."

"I know."

I chewed on my lip, thinking. What about Grandma Greta? She was so sensible, in a soft-edged way. We'd had lots of talks through the years. She'd never once blamed me when she thought I was at fault. She'd just very gently shown me a way to put the situation in focus. "I wonder what Grandma Greta would advise," I ventured.

"What?" Suzy's eyebrows shot up again under the various strands of hair streaming over her face. "She's your dad's mom!"

"Thanks. I know that."

"So can you picture yourself saying, 'These are fine tomatoes, Granny. Oh, by the way, did you know your son has a son you guys have never met? A surprise from the Far East'?"

"I'd bring the subject up in a roundabout way."

"Like?"

"I don't know yet. I'll have to think about it."

I did think about it, all that day and evening. I decided I had to talk to Grandma. I needed some grown-up advice, and she was the only one I knew who could give it. I'd have to be very careful, though, that I didn't make things any worse by talking to her.

❧❧❧❧❧

It worked out perfectly. Grandma said she had to come into the city on Wednesday, and she'd meet me for lunch. That was the day Mom was taking Tyler to the pediatrician for his school checkup.

We met at the entrance to Water Tower Place at eleven thirty. As Grandma walked toward me, the frown between her eyes disappeared. "Alexis, you don't know what this does for my morale, seeing you. I've had a perfectly dreadful time at the dentist's."

"Oh, did he hurt you?"

"Not really. I just don't care for the experience. Are you particularly hungry?"

"No." In fact, I could feel tops spinning where my stomach should be. Was this a good idea after all? What exactly was I going to ask my grandmother?

"Then what do you say we hire one of those horse-drawn carriages to drive us around for a while? That should give us an appetite." She smiled. "But it should give the horse even more of one."

"I've never ridden in a carriage," I said. What a great idea. It would be so much easier to talk to Grandma if I didn't actually have to face her. She used to say that my eyes spoke volumes. Right now I didn't want my eyes to say more than my mouth.

The horse we got was brown and white and was wearing a straw hat with red roses on it. We headed for the side streets and then toward the park.

"Well, dear, what is it you wanted to discuss?" Grandma asked after we'd gone a couple of blocks.

Hesitantly, I said, "It's about a secret. A secret that's gone on for a long time."

"Oh, my."

"And the people that the secret is about have a right to know. At least, that's what I think."

"I see. Then why aren't they being told?" she asked.

"Because . . . the one who could tell wonders if she should. It would be like setting off a string of firecrackers all over the place."

"My goodness. And the person telling would be striking the match that sets off the fireworks?"

"Exactly."

"I see the problem." Grandma turned her head to watch some street entertainers performing on the sidewalk. When we were past them she said, "Let's make sure I've got this right. There's a secret one person knows that another should know. And the one who knows thinks the secret should come out into the open."

"Yes, that's right."

"I'd be inclined to say that the person should just hold back and let things happen as they will."

"But Grandma, there's a kid . . . I mean, another person . . . who knows part of the secret and could screw everything up if he accidentally blabbed."

"Oh, my, this is complicated. I can see why you're concerned."

"So what should I do?" Tears came to my eyes, and my voice faltered.

Grandma took my hand. "Alexis, does this concern your parents?"

"Yes."

"Are they talking divorce? Now don't tell me anything you shouldn't," she said, her voice even lower and huskier than usual. "Just what you need to, right now."

"I haven't heard them talk—" I fumbled for a tissue—"divorce. But they probably will when the secret comes out."

Grandma cleared her throat, and I knew without looking that her eyes were full of concern. "This is a very tough situation for you to be in, my dear. It's not fair for a child."

I swallowed. "I helped make this secret thing happen, and I'm not one bit sorry. It's just that I hate to think what my parents will do when they find out."

"What have you done? Oh, Alexis," Grandma went on, sounding quite concerned, "surely you're not involved with drugs?"

"Drugs?" I could hear the shock in my own voice. "Of course not! This is a grown-up situation. But it's driving me out of my mind because . . ."

She finished my thought. "Because of something you know."

"Right."

"And you want my advice."

"Oh, yes!"

"Alexis, I think you have to tell your parents this secret, whatever it is, and let them sort it out. If they come to blows, so be it. But at least the air will have been cleared."

I breathed a huge sigh and flopped back against the seat. "Thanks, Grandma." She'd lifted a tremendous load from my mind.

When the ride was over, we finally had lunch. I felt so free after our conversation that I began babbling mindlessly about Grandma Lily and her Boy Ty and how she planned to fax letters to soap opera stars.

"It's wonderful that you're so involved with Suzy and her family," Grandma said. "I've always thought it interesting that you should become so close to a . . ."

I glanced up. Why had she stopped so abruptly? She took a sip of water. When I wouldn't look away, she continued, "So close to Suzy. But she's a very likable girl. I'm sure that even if you had to move apart, you'd still be best friends."

It seemed to me that Grandma had shifted away from what she had started to say. Could it be that she knew about Dad's other life and now guessed something was going on about that? If she did, she certainly wasn't going to confide in me—or do anything herself. Grandma listened, but she never butted into others' affairs.

When we left the restaurant, Grandma kissed me and said, "Honey, you do what you think you should. You're a very sensible girl. I have every confidence in you."

"Thanks, Grandma. I'll let you know how it all turns out."

I was sure that wouldn't be necessary, though. The whole family would hear about it. After the sounds of bombs exploding had died down.

❧❧❧❧❧

When I got home, I took a deep breath, called Paul, and asked him to meet me at Dad's on Saturday at eleven o'clock.

"Are you sure that that's the right decision, Alexis? I mean, just to spring it on him like that?"

I wasn't sure of anything, but I said, "I can't see any other way. It's better for us to tell him about you than for him to find out about it later."

"Bite the bullet?"

"Exactly."

After a pause I continued, "I'll set it up with Dad. I won't tell him anything ahead of time. We'll just play it by ear when you two meet."

Paul hesitated but he finally agreed to the plan.

Before I could lose my nerve, I called Dad and asked him if I could come over to his apartment on Saturday morning.

"Sure, honey. I may be working, but you know I always like to have you around."

I told Mom that morning where I was going. My

eyes were glued to the TV at the time because I didn't want any direct looks between us.

"I'm going too," Tyler said.

Before I could object, Mom said, "No, Ty, I want you to look through your things. Put aside the toys that you don't play with anymore, and we'll donate them to a charity."

"I think I need all my things," Tyler said.

"Why?" I asked. "In case you relapse and become a two-year-old again?"

"No!" My brother punched me on the arm. "I have very adult toys. Not like that wind-up merry-go-round of yours that used to play such dorky music."

"Used to?" I rubbed my arm. One of these days, when his reedy little arms got bigger, I'd punch him and see how he liked it. "Did you break my music box, you little creep?"

"It was already broken."

"It was not! Stay out of my room and keep your grubby little hands off my stuff!"

"Off my stuff."

"Stop that!"

Mom glared at us. "Knock it off, both of you. I don't know why you can't get along!"

Without thinking, I said, "It runs in the family."

Bad move. Very bad move. Mom may work in a courtroom, but she takes no prisoners. Looking as if she'd like to mop the floor with me, she sent me to my room. "And stay there!" she commanded.

I closed my door and leaned my head against it. Why couldn't I learn to keep my mouth shut? Would Mom's rage extend beyond the time I was to leave for Dad's, or would she chill? It was nearly ten. Paul might already have left; the long bus ride and then the walk to Dad's place would take him close to an hour. I couldn't leave him to meet Dad alone. Paul was counting on me to bridge the gap between them.

I changed clothes and at about a quarter to eleven, I went to Tyler's room where he and Mom were sorting toys. "I'm going to Dad's now," I said.

Mom gave me a look. I know she hated to give in, but then she'd also hate to have me tell Dad why I couldn't keep my appointment with him. "Don't stay all day," was all she said.

Walking over to Dad's place, shaking inside, I tried to think of what I'd say. There was no way I could prepare for this encounter. Anything could happen. Anything. I felt a little sick to my stomach.

CHAPTER 14

When I reached the door of the townhouse, Dad let me in and then went back to a phone call. In the advertising business weekends didn't mean an awful lot. He waved to me and kept talking while I got more jumpy by the minute. I felt like going and hiding in a closet. When the doorbell rang I would probably scream.

Dad hung up, came over and gave me a hug, and asked what was wrong.

"It's just that someone's coming over that I want you to meet."

"Oh? Can you give me a clue?"

"No. He should be here any minute."

"It's a *he*? This sounds serious. You aren't engaged, are you?" He laughed, patted my shoulder, and went back to his desk.

"Oh, Dad!" I didn't like this kind of kidding when I didn't even have a boyfriend to call my own. In fact, I wasn't in the mood for *any* kind of kidding.

"Dad," I said with a slight quiver in my voice,

"this person is very important. Meeting him may change your life. All our lives."

"Alexis." He put down the pen he'd started to write with. "I think you'd better prepare me a little, before this mysterious stranger arrives."

The doorbell stopped his voice. It froze my blood. A series of tremors started in my legs and moved up my body, making me gasp for air.

"For God's sake!" Dad looked really alarmed. "What is it?"

The bell rang again.

I forced myself to move to the door and yank it open.

Paul, looking pale and worried, tried for a smile but it faded when he saw my face.

"Alexis . . ." He took a step backward. "I'd . . ."

"Come in," I said. Paul's eyes focused somewhere above my head.

"Yes, come in," Dad's voice said behind me. "Whoever you might be."

Paul stepped into the hallway. Sunshine came in through a stained glass window to one side, making rose and green shadows on his white shirt.

"Dad," I found my voice. "This is Paul."

Dad extended his hand, and Paul shook it. "Come in, won't you, Paul?"

We went to the living room and sat down, Paul beside me on the sofa and Dad in a chair opposite.

"I take it you're a friend of my daughter?" Dad said.

"Yes. Yes, I am."

"I see. And how long have you known each other?" I could see from Dad's expression that he wasn't alarmed. How could he be, when Paul looked so unthreatening? But of course he was very puzzled.

"I have a strange story to tell," Paul said. "I looked up Alexis when I came to town to enroll at the university. I knew something about her. And Tyler, of course."

"You did." Dad fixed a look on Paul. "And how did you learn this something about my children?"

What Paul said startled me as much as it did my father. "I hired a detective," he answered.

"You *what*?" Dad almost leaped from the chair.

"It probably seems a very peculiar thing to do, but I had a reason."

Dead silence.

Paul reached into his pocket and pulled out his wallet. He took out a photo, and, trembling, handed it to my father before I could see it.

Dad looked at the photo and his face turned white. "Where did you get this?" he asked. "Who are you anyway?"

"I got it from my mother." Paul nodded toward the photo.

Dad's voice shook as he said, "But this is . . . this is Su Lin!"

"She's my mother."

Dad slumped back in the chair, but he didn't take

his eyes from Paul's face. "Are you . . . are you saying . . . ?"

I looked at Paul. He seemed incapable of speech.

"Paul's your son, Dad," I said. My words, soft yet clear, seemed to be coming from someone else. *This isn't real*, I thought. *This isn't happening.*

It was as if time had stopped. There was absolutely no sound. Then Dad said, "My son?"

"Yes," Paul said, standing. "From long ago . . ."

"My son." Dad's voice sounded so strange. He got up, looked searchingly at Paul, then reached out and folded his arms around him. "I can't believe this!"

They both started crying. I joined them in the tears.

Dad pulled back then. Holding Paul's arms, he said, "I don't understand any of this. And yet I do. I can see Su Lin in your face." He paused. "And I think I can see a little of myself."

"He has your mouth," I said.

"But where . . . how . . . ?" I had never seen my dad so totally bewildered. "Paul, why didn't I *know*?"

"Lost correspondence, I guess. I know Mother wrote to you but you probably didn't get the letters. And if you tried to reach her—"

"Tried! I went wild, trying to locate her! Nothing. Even after I got back to the States, I tried, but no word. Eventually I decided it was hopeless, she was gone forever."

146

"A few months after she went back to her family in China, she had me," Paul said. "Several years later she got a job in Beijing. She'd given up on the hope of ever seeing you again, so she ended the marriage. When I was about twelve she met a business-man and married him. Finally we all moved to San Francisco."

Dad looked at the photo again. "Su Lin, so lovely. I have this same one. Somewhere."

"Really, Dad?" I said. I'd never seen it, of course.

Dad handed back the photo. "She's still in San Francisco?"

"Yes. With Grant, her husband, and their two lit-tle girls."

"I'm just . . . I can't get over this," Dad said. "Hearing about her after all these years. And now to find out that I have a nearly grown son! Have you always known about me?"

"Yes. My mother spoke lovingly of you. All my life I've had a desire to meet my real father."

Dad and Paul embraced again, silently.

"I'm so happy, Dad," I said, getting up and putting my arms around the two of them. "I've always wanted a big brother."

Dad lowered his arms then and looked at me. "And how did you come to find out all this? When even I didn't know?"

Paul put a hand on my shoulder. "I located her school and then found her with the help of a photo the detective managed to get. Here." He pulled out a Polaroid.

"Oh, I hate how I look!" I said. It was taken near the lake, when my hair was blowing.

"You look beautiful," Paul said. "Anyway I hung around the area. When I spotted Alexis with Suzy, I followed them." He turned to me. "I just wanted to see you up close."

"That's when we thought someone was shadowing Suzy," I told Dad.

"And then I knew I had to talk to Alexis," Paul said to Dad.

"We gradually met and started talking," I said. "And one day Paul broke down and told me who he was." I hurriedly added, "It wasn't his fault. I got it out of him."

Dad shook his head. "And to think this was all going on, and I hadn't the slightest idea."

"But isn't it wonderful, Dad?"

"Wonderful doesn't begin to express it. Let's have a soda and try to get to know one another. We have a lot of years to cover, Paul." Dad looked a bit dazed.

We sat around the kitchen table, and Paul described his childhood. "By the way, my mother doesn't know anything about this. I don't want you to think . . ."

"Su Lin would never interfere. Tell me, is she as sweet as I remember her?"

"Well, of course I don't know how she was back

then, but she's very, very nice. She calls herself Linda now."

After the talk had finally run out, we realized it was almost two o'clock and we were starving. "Let's go somewhere and celebrate," Dad said. "You can't imagine what a day this is . . . how I'm feeling."

"I think I can," Paul said, with his slow smile. "I think I can."

We found a restaurant a couple of blocks away that was quiet and peaceful-looking. We slid into a corner booth, with Dad in the middle. He looked from Paul to me and shook his head. "To think that a couple of hours ago, I had no idea!"

"Isn't it great, Dad?" Instinctively we all reached out and held hands.

After we'd given our order to the waitress, Dad said, "Now the question is, where do we go from here?"

That certainly brought on a heavy silence. I guess we were all wondering what would happen next. Most particularly what would happen when Mom found out about this very surprising addition to the family.

CHAPTER 15

Before Paul left us, he gave Dad his phone number. They arranged to meet again as soon as possible.

Dad and I went back to his place and talked for a long time. He was still shaken about having an almost-grown-up son.

"How long have you known about all this?" he asked me.

"I met Paul two or three weeks ago but just found out who he really is last week. It was hard to believe at first."

"Tell me about it," Dad said. "I'm in shock."

"But you're glad, aren't you?"

"Glad? I'm overjoyed." He got a dreamy look in his eyes. "Suddenly those days seem like yesterday."

"I've always wondered what it was like when you worked in Hong Kong," I said.

"It was a whole different atmosphere, a whole different world. I'll try to describe it to you some time." Dad cleared his throat. "But right now, before anything else, I have to go tell your mother about Paul."

"Right now? Couldn't it wait?" I felt frightened about what would happen when Mom exploded. She wouldn't be thrilled, either, about the part I'd played.

"This isn't something we can keep to ourselves, now that we know," Dad said. "It's going to be hard enough as it is."

I knew he was right, but still I wished we could postpone telling Mom.

We walked back to our apartment together. *Let her be gone*, I thought.

When we went in the door, Mom called out from another room, "Honey, is that you?"

Dad and I glanced at each other. "It's both of us," he replied.

Mom came into the room and, seeing our solemn faces, gasped, "Something's happened to Tyler!"

"No, Lorraine," Dad said. "Where is he, by the way?"

"He went to the movies with the Thompsons. Or at least I thought he did."

"Then that's where he is," Dad said. "Lorraine, I have to talk to you. Something very surprising has happened. I wanted you to know right away."

"You're being transferred out of town!" Mom actually looked frantic. Would it bother her, I wondered, if he went away? It seemed like it.

"Not that either. There's no use guessing, Lorraine. This is almost beyond belief."

"What is it? What?"

Dad turned to me. "Alexis, would you excuse us?"

"Huh?" I was the central character here, and now I was supposed to get lost?

"Please," Dad said.

I sighed and started from the room. Mom, I saw, was totally mystified. She didn't have a clue. *But how could she?* I thought. I myself had to wonder if this could really be happening.

I went to my room and tensed, but I couldn't hear a sound. They must have gone to their bedroom and closed the door. Would there be shrieks, howls of rage? Who could predict?

I found I was shaking. *Calm yourself. What will be will be. It's out of your hands. Think of something else.*

There was nothing else.

For possibly the first time in my life I wished Tyler would come banging into the apartment. But all was quiet. Finally, after what seemed like eons, I heard Dad and Mom's voices. I thought they might call out to me to join them, but I heard the front door close.

I waited for a while and then tiptoed (on carpet!) from my room to check out the scene. Mom wasn't in the living room. I went back down the hall and saw her bedroom door was closed. Through the door, I could hear her crying.

I went into the living room and slumped onto the sofa. I sat there for what felt like a long time but was probably only about twenty minutes. Mom finally came out of her room, saw me, and stood in the doorway for a minute. "Tyler's not back yet?"

"No."

She sighed and sat down in an easy chair, then just stared at me across the coffee table. "Your father tells me you know about all this."

"Yes." I started shaking again, but Mom didn't look angry.

"I wish you had told me, but I guess you felt you couldn't."

I swallowed, then said, "I'm always afraid to tell you anything."

"Afraid, Alexis?"

"Y-yes."

Mom actually looked startled. "You're afraid to tell me things?"

I started crying. "I never know what you'll do."

"What I'll do?" Her face crumpled a little. "What do you think I'll do?"

I wiped my palms across my cheeks. "Yell, get mad at me."

Mom looked at me in silence for a moment, and then, "Oh, honey," she said, her voice breaking. "Do I do that?"

"Not . . . not all the time," I said, trying to keep from sobbing.

"Come here." She held out her arms and I went to her and we cried together. Smoothing my hair, she said, "Oh, baby, sometimes I forget that you're still a little girl. You seem so grown-up, so wise."

"I get scared a lot."

"I know, I know." She kissed my forehead and my cheeks. "I just get so wrapped up in my own problems, I forget."

I slumped to the floor by her and leaned my head on her knee. "I know you're worried about Dad and everything. And now, Paul."

Mom was quiet for a few moments and then she said, "I've known about Su Lin for a long time. I thought it was all over and forgotten. I'd forgotten about it at least. But the other day when I was cleaning the closet, I found some things of your father's in an old shoe box. There were pictures of Su Lin that he'd saved."

"Could I see them?"

Weakly, Mom said, "The box is on the floor of the closet."

I went in and looked. One photo was the same as the one Paul had shown us. The other was of Su Lin alone, with a sweet smile and long hair over her shoulders. It was signed, *Love always, Su Lin.*

I put it back and went out to the living room. Mom hadn't moved.

"Mom," I said, "it doesn't mean anything. It's just his past."

"But his past has caught up with him. With us." Softly, Mom started crying. "I know that Buddhist ceremony isn't legal here, but I've wondered if he still feels married to Su-Lin."

I went over and sat on the arm of her chair. "Don't cry, Mom. That part of Dad's life is history. Daddy loves you very much. I know he does."

She leaned her head against me and still cried. "I'm so afraid he'll want to go back to her."

"But Su . . . Linda is married."

"In this day and age that doesn't mean much. People get divorced."

She was right about that. Half the kids in my class had stepparents. "She lives in San Francisco," I said. Not exactly the end of the world, but two thousand miles away.

"I wish I knew, I just wish I knew," Mom said. "Now I'm wondering about moving to the suburbs."

"Wondering?" I pulled away in surprise. "Aren't you sure?"

"I thought I was at first. Then I began thinking that perhaps your father and I could work things out. Move, maybe, but not necessarily out there."

My heart lifted. "You still could. I mean, Paul and everything doesn't have to change our lives."

Mom just shook her head.

We heard someone at the door. She wiped her eyes and I moved back to the sofa. Tyler came in.

Seeing Mom's red eyes, he said, "You shouldn't have worried about me. If I'm a little late, it's just because—"

"It's okay," Mom said.

"No one was worried," I told him.

"What's going on? Did someone die?"

"No, honey," Mom said. "Come give me a kiss."

Tyler obliged and then sat down on the floor. "I stopped downstairs to see Lily because she's been so sad lately. Her heart is broken. Her happiness is shattered."

"Why is that?" Mom asked.

"Because I'm moving."

"Tyler," I said, "you're beginning to sound like Talia and Tangerine. Why don't you give the soaps a rest for a while? Do something else. Teach Lily to play chess."

"There may not be time before we move."

"Go wash your hands, Tyler," Mom said.

"I guess I should. I forgot to at Lily's."

When he was gone, Mom asked me, "How much does he know?"

"Just Paul himself, not who he is."

Getting up, Mom said, "Well, at least someone else in the house has been kept in the dark about this long lost relative." With a sigh she went to the kitchen to begin dinner.

I felt a great sense of relief, now that Mom and Dad both knew about Paul. The secret was a secret no longer. What would happen next? I wished I were a writer, plotting out someone else's life. But this was happening to me, and I had no control over future events.

Slight error. There was one thing I could control. That was to get to Suzy and warn her to never, *never*, NEVER reveal to my parents that she'd known about Paul before they did. I mean, truth is truth, but there's no need to get carried away with it.

CHAPTER 16

The next day, Sunday, I heard my mom on the phone, arranging to meet Dad. It didn't sound as if Tyler and I were invited. Sure enough, we weren't.

"You two can go to the movies," Mom said.

"I don't think it's good for me to see movies two days in a row," Tyler said. "A growing child needs sunshine and fresh air."

In other words, he had his antenna extended, and it told him something was going on with the grown-ups.

"Then walk down to the lake," Mom said irritably. "I don't care. But you can't go alone."

Tyler looked at me.

"Why don't you make friends?" I asked. "Why do you always have to hang out with me?"

"I have a friend. Lily."

"Yes, but you're willing to trade her in for a dog."

Tyler looked at Mom, probably with the idea of getting her to commit once and for all, but she paid no attention to him.

"Oh, come along, then," I said to Tyler. "We'll see if Suzy wants to go to the lake or whatever."

Lily, who was watering plants, seemed surprised to see my brother. "No soaps on today, Boy Ty."

"I know that, but I thought we should spend more time together before I move."

Lily put down the watering pot and began wailing. "You really are going to leave? And then you will forget all about Lily!"

"Not right away, but after a while I guess I will."

Quickly, I said to Lily, "Why don't you come for a walk with us? It's gorgeous out there."

"Yes, Grandma," Suzy said. "Put on your shoes and come along."

Lily pulled a handkerchief from her pocket, wiped her eyes, and looked around for her sneakers.

"Here they are, Lily," Tyler said, pulling them from under the sofa. "I'll help you put them on."

While they were occupied, Suzy half-whispered to me, "What's going on at home?"

"My parents are meeting."

"Wow. I hope they don't end up in the local E.R."

"Come on, they're not going to come to blows. My parents are civilized."

"You don't know what they plan to do?"

"Nope. We'll just have to wait and see."

Lily, now wearing her red and white Reeboks, came along with us, holding Tyler's hand. I guess she'd decided to make the most of these last precious moments with her darling.

We got to North Avenue and headed for the

underpass that led to the beach. It's a good thing we weren't in a rush because Lily has a slow, shuffling walk, and Tyler stopped every time he saw a dog. There were hordes of them out on this sunny afternoon.

"That's a poodle," he explained to Lily.

"You like poodle dog?"

"They say they're very smart, but they look stupid to me, especially with pink bows on their ears."

"What dog is that one over there?" Lily pointed a thin finger.

"German shepherd."

"Big."

"Yeah. That black dog's a lab. And that kind of orange one's a golden retriever. The best."

"You know very much about dogs," Lily said.

"You could say that." Tyler looked smug. "I make it a practice to be well informed."

Not about everything, buddy, I thought.

❧❧❧❧❧

When we got back there was a note taped to Suzy's door. It said: *Alexis and Tyler, please come home now.*

I felt panicky. This was the first time Mom had ever left a message like this. Was there an emergency?

"What's up?" Suzy asked.

"I haven't a clue." I grabbed Tyler's shoulder. "Come on."

"Call me!" Suzy yelled as my brother and I headed for the stairs.

My heart was racing. Now what? Tyler was clattering behind me, whining, "What's the big rush?"

I waited for him to catch up with me at the foot of the stairs and again when we got to the door of our apartment. I stood there, breathing heavily. What was on the other side of that door? I was afraid something bad was about to be revealed and I wasn't ready.

I wasn't ready, either, for the sight that greeted me. Both Mom and Dad were in the living room, but that wasn't all. Paul was seated on a chair facing them!

As I stood in the doorway with my mouth hanging open, Tyler rushed past me and raced over to Paul. "Hey! Paul! What are you doing here?"

I gave Mom a swift look. She didn't seem a bit angry. In fact, she had a smile. It was a small smile, but it was there all the same.

"You've met," I said, rather stupidly.

Paul gently put Tyler aside, stood, and, coming over, gave me a hug. "We've met," he said. "Thanks to you."

Again I glanced at Mom. She didn't have the dreaded *We'll talk about this later* expression. In fact she seemed a little unsure of herself, which wasn't her usual style. With the small smile still on her face, she kept looking from one of us to the other. Finally she settled on my brother.

"Tyler," she said, "please sit down. Paul has something to tell you."

We all sat down.

Here it comes, I thought. How would Paul break the news? Would he begin with Dad's days in Hong Kong?

Paul glanced at each of us in turn and then to Tyler said simply, "I'm your half brother."

In my mind I will always carry the snapshot of Tyler's expression. He was without words for the first time since learning to talk. His eyes were round as golf balls behind the little rimmed glasses.

"Br-brother!" Tyler finally gasped. "I don't understand!"

"Aren't you glad?" I asked.

For answer, he leaped at Paul, not understanding but not caring. "It's stupendous!" Then, becoming more himself, he added, "I'm not really surprised, you know. I sensed it all along."

I rolled my eyes the way Suzy often does.

While Tyler hung onto Paul, Dad took over, giving a condensed version of the family history.

When he'd finished, my brother twisted his head around to look at Paul. "Are you going to move in with us?"

"No." Paul laughed. "I have a room out at the university. I'll be busy with studies, but I hope to see you often." He shot a look at Mom. "Not so often you'll wish I'd go away again."

"Nonsense," Mom said. "You're part of the family now, Paul. We want you to come visit us whenever you can."

Wow. Did she mean it or was she just racking up brownie points? I couldn't tell.

After a while Paul made moves to leave, but both my parents insisted he stay for dinner. Dad said he'd take us all out, but Mom said no, she'd cook.

I was setting the table at the end of the living room when I thought of Suzy. She must be in a real state, wondering what was going on. I'd have liked to ask if she could come and join us for dinner, but I didn't want to destroy the circle of family togetherness.

I did slip away to my room to call and give her the news. Suzy's squeals nearly shattered my eardrums. "I can't believe it!" she said after I revealed each little nugget. "It's like a fairy tale! No, better, because it's real."

"Suzy, I've got to go now. We're all going to have dinner together. I'll bring you up to speed when I see you."

"On the way to school tomorrow!"

School. I'd forgotten about it starting. "Yes, tomorrow," I said.

Dinner was surprisingly normal. Well, at first there was a little strain, this being the first time we were all together. After a while, though, the conversation centered on Paul's studies and what he hoped to do in life.

He said he'd been drawn to Chicago because of its architectural history. He wanted to study the works of the past and then experiment with his own ideas for buildings of the future.

Then he turned to Mom and said, "Look, I'm just beginning my career. But I'd really like to hear about yours. Does the job get to you sometimes?"

"Like how?"

"Do you ever feel sorry for the defendants when they're cross-examined? Do you wish you could help them out?"

"I have to stay neutral," Mom said. "I just concentrate on getting all the words down. Sometimes, though, I feel sorry for people who seem trapped by life." She'd never gone on about her job to us, but she and Paul had quite a conversation. I glanced at Dad, and he seemed pleased that they were getting along so well.

At about nine o'clock Paul got ready to leave. Everyone hugged him and made him promise to come back soon, with Tyler overdoing it, of course.

After he'd gone, Mom turned to Dad and asked, "Are you leaving too?"

"You want me to?"

Mom hesitated. "I want you to stay, but it's up to you."

"I'll stay then."

164

"Forever, Dad?" Tyler asked.

"Go get ready for bed," Mom told him. "School tomorrow."

I told the folks I'd clean up the dishes. While I cleared the table, they went over to the sofa and began to talk. From the kitchen I could look through the cutaway wall to the living room. I tried to hear what they were saying out there, but Mom had put some Beethoven on the CD player—I guess to block out their voices. Well!

I'd stowed all the dishes in the washer and was starting on the pans when the disc ended.

Mom's voice came through. "I've often wondered how much you regretted losing her."

"Lorraine, I got over Su Lin a long time ago," Dad said. "That's the past. You're the one I married for keeps. I've never—"

And then Mom glanced my way. I turned out the kitchen light, called out good night, and went to my room. Goodbye, eavesdropping.

When I went to bed, they were still talking out there, with background music once again. I tried to think about school starting, but my mind kept going to Hong Kong and what it must have been like for Dad and Su Lin being in love and being separated. And how he gave up finally and started a new life back home with his high school sweetheart.

He'd said a while ago that he had gotten over his

life with Su Lin. But had he really forgotten how much he loved her?

A shocking thought came to me. Had Paul told his mother about us? If so, what about her feelings for Dad? Would she want to see him again? I felt shivery and shaky.

As I was putting my blue headband into the drawer, I noticed a crumpled piece of paper in a corner. I unfolded it and read, *The things you wish for most you can achieve.* My fortune. When I'd first read it I had thought it was a lot of jargon. How could I achieve anything? But now there was hope.

I smoothed out the paper and read it again. Would my fortune cookie lie?

CHAPTER 17

"Isn't it great," Suzy said the next day at school, "that you can start the term with everything at home all settled?" We were in the locker room, changing for Phys Ed. "Now we can concentrate on important things."

"I take it you don't mean schoolwork," I said. "But things aren't totally settled at home."

"How come? You said your mom liked Paul. What did she call him? Highly intelligent and sensitive? That's top praise, coming from her."

I got up from the bench and stood beside Suzy as we both looked into the long mirror. "Mom likes Paul all right. I mean, who wouldn't? But that's just one thing. There's other stuff I'm worried about."

"Like?" Suzy licked her thumb and finger and straightened out a strand of her bangs.

"Dad hasn't moved back home yet."

"He will, though, won't he?"

I shrugged. "It seems like he might. But you never know about parents."

"He will," Suzy said. "He's really tied up with

your family. He's crazy about all of you. I can tell."

"Then there's the other thing," I said, pulling my hair into a ponytail and fastening on a barrette. "When Linda—that's Su Lin—finds out about us, she might decide to get Dad back. Remember, they were crazy about each other years ago."

"People change." Suzy leaned toward the mirror to check a possible zit.

"Or," I went on, "she might be wildly jealous and not want Paul to associate with us."

"Alexis, you're just looking for trouble. Come on, let's head for the soccer game and do battle."

I followed Suzy out of the locker room, thinking that in spite of what she'd said, our battles at home could be just beginning.

❦❦❦❦❦

When I walked into the apartment that afternoon, Mom seemed to be waiting for me.

"Alexis, please come sit down," she called from the living room. "I want to talk with you."

Oh, man, I thought. *She's finally going to blast me for knowing about Paul and not coming to her.* I might have known that eventually she would.

"What's up?" I asked as casually as I could.

"I've been thinking about our conversation the other day. About how little we talk to each other about important things."

I didn't know what to say so I said nothing.

"Like moving to the suburbs, for instance," she said.

My heart gave a lurch. *Here it comes.*

"I realize that I went ahead with my plans without really talking it over with the family. Of course, your dad knew. . . ."

"So did Tyler. You promised him a dog."

Mom smiled weakly. "And lived to regret it."

"You should have told me," I mumbled.

"Yes, I should have. I'm truly sorry, Alexis. You said not long ago that you were afraid to tell me things. I guess I sometimes feel the same way about you."

"*Me?*" My mother was afraid of *me*?

"You're so intense sometimes. So emotional in your own quiet way. I guess I thought it would be easier for me to go ahead and make the move and then deal with you. I realize now that that was the totally wrong way to handle it."

I felt a catch in my throat. "Mom, I've been so upset."

Mom sighed and pulled me close to her on the sofa. "I wish I'd done it differently. I should have been up front with you."

Her words should have reassured me, but she hadn't really answered the big questions I had. I forced myself to ask, "Have you and Dad decided? I mean, what you're going to do?"

"About us, or about moving?"

"Both."

"No. We haven't."

I pulled away and sat up straight. "You know he wants to stay in the city."

"Of course I know that."

"So couldn't you . . . ?"

After a pause, Mom said, "Since it means so much to him—well, I guess we could work something out. If he still . . ." She swallowed.

"If he still *what*?"

Mom didn't answer. I turned to look at her. She was biting her lips.

"Mom?" She had the strangest look on her face. "What's the matter?"

She swallowed again and said, "It's just that he loved her so very much."

"That was a long time ago. He loves you now. I know he does."

"Yes, I want to believe that . . ."

We heard a key in the lock, and Tyler burst into the room. Great timing, as always.

"Ready, Mom? To go get my gym shoes?" he asked.

"Oh, Tyler, can't it wait? Your father's coming over."

"Mom! I need them tomorrow. You promised!"

Mom looked at her watch, went to the kitchen, and checked a casserole in the oven. Then she picked up her purse and asked me to tell Dad they'd be home within the hour. I had the feeling that it was good our conversation had ended. What else was there to say?

~~~~~~~~

When Dad walked in, I decided to check out what was on his mind. After giving him Mom's message, I followed him into the kitchen where he put a cup of cold coffee into the microwave.

"Dad," I began, "do you want to see Su Lin again?"

"Not particularly," he said. I wished I could see his expression, but his back was toward me. "The past is the past."

"Don't you still have feelings for her?"

"I have memories. That's enough. They have nothing to do with my feelings for you and Tyler."

I trembled a little but still asked, "What about Mom?"

"Your mother is my wife. That will never change."

"But do you still love her, Dad?"

He gave me a quick look. "Of course I do. What a question!" Then he added, with a one-sided smile, "I just wish she were a little easier to get along with at times."

"Like Suzy's mother?"

"What? Oh, no. She's a nice lady, but I'm afraid I'd find her a little dull. No fire."

"Well, Dad, you can't have it both ways. If you

like Mom's fire, you have to take the heat some-times."

He laughed. "You're quite the little philosopher. When did you say she'd be back?"

I followed him as he took his coffee to the dining room table. "About an hour." I sat down, too, think-ing this could be my one chance to sound him out.

Dad reached for the morning paper that was lying on the table and opened it to the Arts Section.

"I don't think Mom's so set now on moving to Medsville," I said.

"Hmmm? What makes you think so?"

"She said maybe we could work things out. About the move, I mean."

"I sincerely hope so." He was reading a review of a play.

"But I think she's afraid of losing you."

Dad looked up. "What? That's absurd."

"Well, you did leave home, you know." And with those words it suddenly came to me that Dad was at fault sometimes too. It wasn't always Mom. "You could have talked it over with Mom instead of just taking off."

"I could have. Probably should have." Dad put down the paper and looked at me. "Alexis, I hate to say this, but parents aren't perfect. They don't always do the right thing."

I looked down and picked at my fingernail. "So what's going to happen next?" I hoped he'd say he was going to move back home and that we probably wouldn't move, but he only said, "We'll have to wait and see."

❦❦❦❦

If I'd thought things would be settled that night, I was wrong. When Mom came home, she and Dad talked. But there was still a little strain in their voices.

Dad did stay for dinner, and for once I was glad of Tyler's babbling, since it helped ease the tension.

Suddenly he announced, "I told all the kids at school about the dog I'm getting."

Great, I thought.

Mom and Dad exchanged quick looks and then Mom said, "Baby, I've been thinking. Maybe we should hold off on the dog for a while."

"What?" Tyler's fork fell to the plate with a clatter. "You said I could get one just as soon as we moved!"

"Well, yes, but I'm not sure when that will be. We may change our plans," Mom said.

"And shatter all my dreams?" Tyler shrieked.

"Come off it," I said. "Spare us the high drama."

Dad put a hand on Tyler's shoulder. "Calm down, son," he said. "We'll work something out."

My brother sniffed and picked up his fork. "A boy really needs a dog," he said. I rolled my eyes, and

Dad and Mom smiled at each other and shook their heads. At that moment I felt the tension between them ease.

"There's something else we should talk about," Mom said. "We have a party to plan."

"Party?" We all looked at her.

"Your grandparents are dying to meet Paul," she said. "So let's do it."

"Wow!" Tyler said. "Do they know he's my new brother?"

"Yes, of course," Dad said. "How about a dinner party this weekend? We could go somewhere special."

"Let's do it here," Mom said.

"Can—may Suzy come too?" I asked. "She knows about Paul." I wasn't dumb enough to say how much she knew and that they'd already met.

"Sure, invite Suzy," Dad said. "She's like part of the family."

I glanced at Mom. She smiled in agreement.

Tyler set down his glass of milk. "Do you think Grandpa and Grandma will like Paul better than me?"

I groaned. "Impossible, Ty. You're in a class by yourself." I remembered, though, my fears when Tyler was born that my parents would love the new baby more than me.

"Every person," Dad had said then, "is loved in a special way. Love is not a competitive sport."

Now I realized more than ever what that meant. Dad had loved Su Lin. But that didn't mean he couldn't love Mom now, today. Each had a special place in his life.

ෲෲෲෲ

Suzy wasn't as excited as I thought she'd be when I told her about the dinner invitation. "I guess you've forgotten that that's the night we celebrate the Moon Festival."

"We? Meaning who?"

"My aunts are coming in from Chinatown. I guess they'll bring the mooncakes."

"Which you hate. Well, celebrate your festival, then. We'll just have dinner without you."

"Since you insist, I'll just do both," Suzy said. "Don't forget to introduce me to Paul. Remember, we've supposedly never met."

I was pretty sure that in all the excitement no one would even notice.

That night, when I was getting ready for bed, I saw the little scrap of paper from the fortune cookie again. *The things you wish for most you can achieve.* I was getting close. But now with the Moon Festival coming up, I'd be sure to offer up the ashes of my fortune to the moon. It couldn't hurt to go that extra distance.

CHAPTER 18

We blew up big bunches of balloons and hung them everywhere. The table was set with our best china, and we put a bouquet of fall flowers in the center.

Tyler was so excited his voice squeaked. "Shouldn't we make a banner that says 'Welcome, Paul'?"

"He's already been here," I objected.

"Oh, well," Mom said, "go to your room and make one, Tyler." I could tell he was getting on her nerves.

My brother dashed off, and Mom went back to the kitchen to check on the food. Dad got out wine glasses, and I put them on the table. We had set a place for Suzy, but she wasn't sure when she would arrive.

The doorbell rang. Tyler, crayon in hand, dashed out and pressed the intercom before anyone else could get there. "It's Grandma and Grandpa," he said, buzzing them in.

They arrived with another vase of flowers, which

Grandma put on the coffee table. "I see he's not here yet," she said.

"Any minute." Mom came out of the kitchen.

I noticed a special look pass between her and my grandparents when they hugged. It seemed to say they were glad that the disagreements had been settled.

"Grandpa," Tyler said, burrowing in between them, "if there were thirty birds sitting on—"

"Put it in retirement," I said. "That's such an old one."

"—sitting on a telephone wire, and someone shoots four, how many would be left?"

"You shouldn't shoot birds," I said.

Tyler ignored me. "None! The rest of them flew away!" He paused. "Get it, Grandpa? The noise from the—"

The buzzer rang. Tyler ran and talked into the intercom. "It's Paul!" he shouted. "Paul!"

We all stood like a congregation, waiting for the final blessing. Then Mom moved Tyler aside and opened the door, ready to welcome Paul.

He hesitated outside for a moment, then came into the room. Mom took his arm. "Paul, here are your grandparents," she said. Dad moved to his other side.

For just a moment they looked at each other. Then Grandma Greta went to Paul, took hold of his hands, and said, "It's wonderful to see you, my dear.

At last. We've been waiting all week for this moment."

"Me, too," Paul said, finding his voice.

"I'm Greta, and this is your Grandpa Mac."

The men shook hands. Then Grandpa said, "Oh, shoot," and put his arms around Paul. "It's great to have you in the family."

Paul's eyes looked a little moist. "I'm really glad to be here. With all of you."

"I was going to make a sign," Tyler said, "that said 'Welcome, Paul.' But I didn't have time, so I'll just say it. WELCOME, PAUL!"

Mom shushed him, then said, "Why don't you all sit down over there and get acquainted?"

"I'll pour the wine," offered Dad. "Why wait? Come on, Alexis, you can help."

I took the glasses off the table and into the kitchen where Dad was opening the bottle. His hands shook as he poured a little into each wine glass. "A month ago," he said, "who'd have thought we'd be having a celebration like this?"

"Right," I agreed. Not too long ago I'd been thinking that if and when the family got together it would be like a rerun of the Battle of Gettysburg.

As I carried in the glasses—my hands were shaking, too—everyone was talking about Paul's classes. He seemed very earnest, more serious than before, but pretty much at ease. My grandparents had accepted him so warmly that he had lost his earlier nervousness.

178

"What branch of architecture are you most interested in?" Grandpa was asking. "Or is too soon to decide?"

"Well, not commercial buildings, and probably not homes," Paul said. "I think I'd like to do cultural structures in conjunction with parks, but . . ." He paused to take the glass I was holding out for him. "We'll see."

"I guess you'd better bring me a Pepsi," Tyler said after I had served the adults.

"I guess you'd better go get it yourself," I said.

Tyler stomped toward the kitchen but swerved to the door when a knock sounded.

It was Suzy.

"Oh, you've already met each other," she said, looking a bit disappointed over missing the grand reunion. She smiled at my grandparents.

"Suzy, this is Paul," I said hurriedly.

"Wow! Glad to meet you!" She rushed over and shook his hand while he looked a bit puzzled. "I've heard so much about you!"

"Same here," Paul said, recovering.

"Let's go get Lily!" Tyler said. "She'd like to meet Paul, too, I bet!"

"She's not home," Suzy said. "My aunts couldn't make it to the celebration after all, so Lily left. Maybe she went to get some mooncakes." Suzy sat down on the floor, and I sat beside her. Tyler scooted between us, worried, as always, that he might miss something.

"Paul," Grandma said, "how do your parents feel about all this? Or do they know?"

"Oh, they know. I think they're really glad that I have family here. My mother especially was concerned about my moving so far from home." He smiled. "You know how mothers are. Anyway, they know about tonight and asked if we could take pictures. But I don't have a camera."

"We do," Dad said, and nodded to me.

I got up and took the Pentax from a shelf. It already had film in it.

Paul reached into his jacket pocket. "I brought a few photos. I thought you might like to see my sisters and everyone."

Everyone. I looked at Dad but couldn't read his expression.

"Here's Kristie," Paul said, holding out a snapshot. "And Laura. She's a handful."

"She's adorable," Grandma said. "They both are." She passed the photos around.

"And here's my mom and dad," Paul said.

Mom, biting her lips, took the photo and then seemed to relax. "She's . . . they're . . . very nice looking," she said. She handed the photo to Dad.

I guess we were all looking at him. He stared at the photo, blinked, and nodded. "She's changed."

"It's been a long time," Grandma said. She held out her hand for the photo, and I scrambled to look over her shoulder.

What a surprise! This Linda looked so different from the Su Lin of the earlier picture. Her hair was cut short, she wore glasses, and, well, she looked a lot older. I glanced over at Dad, who caught my look and nodded toward the camera still in my hand. I went over and gave it to him.

"How are we going to do this?" he asked. "All together or singly or what?" His voice was a little shaky.

"Why not get lots of shots?" Suzy asked. "If you want, I'll take them so you can all be together."

She took one picture of the whole bunch and then several of separate groups. While she was setting up one with the grandparents, Mom went out to the kitchen. I followed.

"Mom, are you all right?" I asked as she leaned against the counter, braced by her hands.

"Alexis." She swallowed. "It's just . . . so upsetting . . . after all this time."

"He doesn't love her anymore," I said. "That's all over. He loves you best. I'm sure he always has."

"Oh, sweetheart," she said. "I know that. But it's nice to hear you say it."

We started putting food on the table. Tyler had control of the camera now and was taking pictures like crazy. He finally stopped, only because he'd finished the roll.

The grown-ups brought their wine glasses to the

table and toasted the occasion. The rest of us, including Paul, did the same with soda.

It wasn't until the meal was over and the dishes cleared that I remembered the moon wish I was going to make. I got the paper fortune, took a saucer and matches, and went out on the balcony. Suzy followed.

"What are you doing?"

"Making sure my fortune comes true." I touched the flame to the paper, and in seconds it was ashes. I lifted the saucer and blew what remained of my fortune to the moon.

"Where did you get that idea?" Suzy asked with a frown.

I stared. "From *you*, bogus brain!"

"Me? Are you sure?"

"Suzy, you are so dense. Don't you remember telling me to do this to make my fortune come true?"

"No. I must have made it up."

"Oh!" I suddenly understood Tyler's need to punch me on the arm. It was all I could do to keep from whacking Suzy.

"What did your fortune say?" she asked.

"The things you wish for most you can achieve."

Grandma Greta came out to the balcony. "Suzy, honey, would you mind if I spoke to Alexis for a moment?"

"Of course not." Suzy left.

"It's a beautiful night, isn't it?" Grandma looked up at the full moon. "A beautiful night in so many ways."

"It certainly is," I said with a sigh.

"Alexis," Grandma began, "do you remember when we had that talk, the day we rode in the carriage?"

"Yes, I do. I was really upset."

"I know you were. But you did the right thing, honey, to go to your parents and tell them what was going on."

"It was about Paul."

"I thought so. And it was certainly something they needed to know."

Everyone drifted out to the balcony then.

"Just look at that moon." It gave Mom's face a glow. "And you can see it shimmering on the lake, there in the distance."

I couldn't help saying, "I would miss this view so much if we moved."

"Our new place will have just as good a view," Dad assured us.

"What?" Several of us spoke together.

"We were going to tell you later, but why wait?" Dad said. "Tell them, Lorraine."

"We've found a wonderful apartment not far from here. It's within walking distance for you two girls, and it has a guest bedroom for Paul."

We were all too surprised to speak. Then Tyler wailed, "What about me and my dog?"

Dad laughed. "They allow pets in the new building, Tyler. Now, is everyone happy?"

We were all talking at once, asking question after question, when suddenly there was a loud knock at the door. Surprised, suddenly silent, we turned, but Tyler was already dashing inside. The next thing we heard was a yell. Then wild barking, yips, and scuffling sounds.

We rushed inside to see a golden retriever circling like mad, barking, with Lily trying to hold onto its leash. "Dog! Dog!" she cried out. "Not so fast!" She let go, and the dog dashed over to Tyler. Still yapping, he slobbered kisses on Tyler's face and neck.

"Dog knows you!" exclaimed Lily. "I told him Boy Ty would be very happy to see him. Looks like dog is happy too."

Tyler managed to get his face away from the dog's wild and wet kisses. "Is he yours, Lily?"

"No, it is for you, Boy Ty. Now you do not have to move to get dog. You got one already."

"But we're still going to move," Tyler told her. "Not far, though, Lily." He shielded his face from more licks by the dog. "I know what! When I walk him, I'll bring him over to your apartment. Twice a day!"

"Okay." Lily's worried expression changed to a smile.

"You're my witness," I murmured to Suzy. "Tyler's going to walk that hound. Not me."

"We can all do it," said Suzy. "It'll be fun. Come

on, Ty. Let's give him a road test. Well, sidewalk. Want to go, Lily?"

"No, you come see me downstairs when you get back."

"Alexis?"

"Not now." I knew, in spite of Tyler's promises, that there'd be plenty of times I'd be stuck with walking the dog. Besides, I didn't want to leave the party.

After Lily, Suzy, Tyler, and the dog left, our apartment seemed very quiet.

"This is certainly a full night," Grandma said, "and I'm not referring to the moon. First we meet our wonderful new grandson, another grandson gets his dog, and then there's the surprising news about the move. When did this new apartment come into the picture? My word, you folks move fast."

"We just went out and did it," explained Dad. "It seemed the perfect solution. We were lucky to find a great place right away."

"So, Paul," Grandpa said, "there's no excuse for you to stay a stranger. You'll have your own room here in the city and we certainly have a place for you in Medsville."

"It's nice out there," I told Paul. "It's where our roots are, isn't it, Mom . . . Dad?" What was I saying? Did I really believe that?

When I thought about it, I realized that I did. Not that I wanted to go back there and live. That hadn't changed. But a part of me was there, where my grandparents lived, where my parents had lived, and where I had, too, for a time, nearby.

I looked at Paul. Were his roots in San Francisco or in China? Would they ever grow here, among us? Just then he turned to me and smiled. He had found his new place, at least for a while. We'd enjoy being together, my new brother and I, for as long as we could.

Life is not made of wishes, I thought as I glanced around our living room. It's made up of love. And it looked as if all of us had enough of that to keep us going for a very long time.